THE SWEET REDEMPTION OF
REPREHENSIBLE BOB

THE SWEET REDEMPTION OF REPREHENSIBLE BOB

A Hollywood Satire about One Man's
Obsession with Breasts and One Woman's
Unquenchable Thirst for Revenge

DAVID CREPS

The Sweet Redemption of Reprehensible Bob
A Hollywood Satire about One Man's Obsession with Breasts and One Woman's Unquenchable Thirst for Revenge

Published by Boogie Woogie Books and David Creps
ISBN: 978-1-7354725-0-8

This book is dedicated to all those, beginning with my grandmother, who preempted some looming complaint about my behavior, by saying, "Okay. What's he done now?"

CHAPTER ONE

In 1978, seated at a desk in the front row of her first-grade class, a cute little girl with large, horn-rimmed glasses, raised her hand.

The teacher acknowledged the girl, and she stood and answered the question that had stumped the rest of the class.

Not only was she the smartest student in her school, Margaret Bennington was also the most responsible. She willingly did chores for her allowance and had a savings account into which she put small amounts of money each and every week without fail.

She was also the most popular.

Margaret could often be seen swinging in the school playground with an eager group of classmates gathered around her, vying for the privilege of being the one to push her swing while basking in the wonderful smile she was always ready to give those who sought her friendship.

As she grew older, her sphere of influence expanded to include people from many different walks of life.

In 1989, she got her first job: 'running' the front counter at a local burger joint where construction workers, police officers, business executives, military personnel, postal employees, etc.–stood at the counter and gave the teenage girl wearing the big, horn-rimmed glasses their undivided attention as she made change and 'handed off' burgers and fries. Later, within the halls of serious academia, Margaret Bennington was considered to be uncommonly brilliant and was often singled out for praise, asked to join clubs, and urged to run for political office.

And it was she alone, amongst all her friends, who retained her virginity throughout high school, college, and beyond, steadfastly saving herself for the man of her dreams, her soul-mate, the one with whom she would marry and raise children.

In the spring of 1999, looking resplendent in her cap and gown, a remarkably poised young woman wearing large, horn-rimmed glasses, stood at a lectern and spoke into a microphone as she delivered the valediction at the Harvard University graduation ceremony.

Margaret planned to have a spiritually fulfilling, financially rewarding, and very glamorous career. Hence, she set out to become the most influential Christian media personality in the world–so that she could cast her heartfelt values far and wide.

She had, once and for all, confidently put her future in the hands of the Lord.

There was no end to her goodness, no limit to her intellectual aptitude, and no flaw in her character . . . aside from what might be considered a somewhat irrational fear of spiders.

CHAPTER TWO

On September 7th, 1999, in a very plush corporate office of an Atlanta skyscraper, a group of executives was gathered at an oblong table for an important meeting. An FXN logo made of silver letters protruding from a slab of shiny black marble covered one entire wall of the room.

The CEO sat at the head of the table and spoke: "So, after our fifth straight month of a diminishing market share among viewers between thirty-five and sixty, I have decided to make a major change in the way FXN will present the news.

"For the future, I intend to give it an entirely new look. More sophisticated in style. A little more cosmopolitan in approach. And at the same time, we are going to give a more intellectually challenging and culturally nuanced slant to our Christian-based editorial positions.

"And so, to that end, after reading the resumes and viewing the audition tapes of literally hundreds upon hundreds of possible candidates to symbolize this new look . . .

"I have chosen someone who is so obviously head and shoulders above all the other applicants that I feel fortunate beyond measure to soon have the distinct privilege of being able to say: 'I am the one who first brought her into our industry.'"

An enthusiastic murmur from around the table echoed after the CEO's last remark.

The CEO continued, "And I have called you up here today so that you will all have a chance to see for yourselves the charm, the charisma, and the intelligence that is going to symbolize the future of FXN news."

At this point, an intercom pinged, and a voice was heard: "Ms. Bennington is in the lobby and on her way up."

The CEO stood up from his chair. "So, now I think it only fitting that this company's CEO, and its entire Board of Directors, meet her at the elevator and give this lovely young lady from Minneapolis a big warm Southern welcome."

The Board of Directors joined the CEO as he walked out of the office and across a wide hallway. The group then positioned itself in front of the elevator doors, with each gentleman discreetly preening as he prepared to make his first impression upon this important new media star.

In the lobby of the FXN skyscraper, a fashionably attired woman wearing large glasses and carrying a briefcase stepped into the elevator and pushed the button for the thirty-ninth floor.

Before the doors closed, Robert Gerald Longpooper–a young man with a very large nose–stepped inside, smiled, and nodded, "Hello."

The elevator began to go up, with the lights on the buttons indicating the speed of ascension. As the lights hit six, seven, and eight, the woman became increasingly aware that the man standing beside her was focused on her breasts.

She turned slightly to address him. "Excuse me?"

Robert seemed genuinely upset about something, and shyly indicated to the front of her blouse.

The woman expressed her growing annoyance: "Excuse me?"

Again, Robert indicated to the front of her blouse. And because there was a definite urgency in this seemingly shy person's demeanor, the woman's annoyance turned to concern.

"What?" she asked.

Robert indicated down the inside of his own shirt.

The woman raised her voice. "What?"

Robert drew in a deep breath. "A spider."

"A spider?! Down my blouse?!"

Robert nodded. "Yes."

The woman dropped her briefcase and slapped at her blouse, yelling for help. "Get it! Get it off me!"

Robert stepped forward and reached into her blouse as the

elevator buttons lit up the fourteenth and then the fifteenth floor.

The woman held her arms back so as not to impede Robert's efforts. She had become hysterical. "Get it! Hurry! Please hurry!"

Robert unbuttoned the woman's blouse, spread it apart, and looked inside.

"Get it! Get it!" she shouted.

Robert shook his head. "I'm sorry. It must have crawled into your bra."

As the buttons lit up the twentieth and twenty-first floors, the woman's hysteria intensified. "Hurry! Before it bites me! Get it!"

Robert reached first into one side of her bra and withdrew a breast, which he was quickly able to examine for spiders by holding it upward by its nipple.

"Please hurry!" she wailed.

With his other hand, Robert reached into her bra and withdrew her other breast, and after some slight manipulation, ascertained that it too was spider-free. "Maybe it crawled down into your pants."

She shrieked. "Get it out! Get it out!"

Robert dropped to his knees, unzipped her pants, pulled them down, and began to frantically brush off all areas between her breasts and her knees.

On the thirty-ninth floor, the group of executives antici-pation grew as they waited at the elevator doors, ready to get their first glimpse of the woman who will symbolize the future of FXN News. With a *ding*, the doors opened, and there stood a woman spasmodically shaking and jittering every part of her body while screaming at the man on his knees in front of her who had his arms stretched around her mid-section and was slapping wildly at her buttocks as she screamed, "I feel it! I feel it!"

And then, the elevator doors closed, followed by a complete lack of sound or movement from the slack-jawed executives.

And as a direct result of this unfortunate incident, Margaret Bennington immediately moved far out into the Nevada desert and became a chicken farmer.

CHAPTER THREE

Robert Gerald Longpooper, the shy gentleman slapping imaginary spiders from Margaret's buttocks, was, from earliest childhood–shall we say–oddly programmed. Assorted incidents of this nature were not wholly unfamiliar to him.

In 1976, in a small Brooklyn apartment, on a well-worn couch, amid many religious paintings and small plastic statues of babies suckling at their mothers' breast, Angela, a thoroughly overwhelmed Catholic woman had a baby with an unusually large nose suckling at her breast. Five children, all under ten years of age, were running wildly around the room.

Before long, she turned to her husband–who was drinking beer and listening to the Dodgers' baseball game on a small radio in the kitchen–and spoke with a huff of exasperation, "Frank. For God's sake. Do something."

Without diverting his attention from the radio, Frank responded, "What can I do?"

She rocked the baby back and forth, constantly adjusting her position to keep his large nose from causing too much discomfort. "Something. Anything. Don't just sit there. Call your mother and ask her what to do."

Frank, still without diverting his attention from the radio, picked up the phone and called his mother.

She answered, "Hello."

"It's me, Ma."

Angela could hear Frank's mother's startled gasp from across the room. "Frankie? You called. Oh my God, what's happened?!"

"Don't worry, Ma, nobody died. I just gotta ask ya sumpin'."

"Frankie, with God as my witness, I swear on your dear father's grave, in the name of all that is holy, I–"

"Ma! Stop! For God's sake, it's only a question!"

"Okay, Frankie, my oldest son, your mother is listening."

"The baby won't quit suckin' on Angela's boobs. How do we get 'im offa' der'?"

And so it was that Robert Longpooper gained an early reputation, at least within his family, as a serious "breast man."

* * *

As an adolescent, Robert's favorite cartoon character was the cute little French skunk, Pepe Le Pew, which, for a few years, inspired him to wear a beret and speak with a goofy sounding French accent. And occasionally, a female adult would call him "a charming young man." However, as he grew older, Robert Longpooper's stylish French charm was often misunderstood.

On a bright summer day in 1982, on a beach at Lake Tahoe with numerous swimmers and sunbathers, a six-year-old boy with a large nose, wearing a Cub Scout uniform and a French beret, walked toward two senior citizens (a husband and his wife) sitting on the beach eating sandwiches. The husband watched the young boy approach.

The boy, whose name-badge identified him as Robert Longpooper, walked past the husband and stood in front of the wife. He then stretched out his hand and spoke, "Le yum yum?"

The wife, mistaking him for a mentally disabled child, thought he was asking for a sandwich. She smiled and said, "Of course." She then reached into the ice chest, pulled out a sandwich, and offered it to him. "Yum yum. Peanut butter and jelly."

The young boy reached out, but instead of taking the sandwich, he placed his hand inside her bathing suit and took hold of a breast. The husband was stunned into momentary disbelief, but then immediately jumped up to defend his wife's honor.

"What the hell do you think you're doing, you perverted little bastard!?" he shouted.

The boy let go of the breast, withdrew his hand from the bathing suit, and walked off.

Spittle flew from the husband's mouth. "You ever come back here again, I'll kick your ass! Do you hear me?! You perverted little French son-of-a-bitch!

* * *

The older Robert got, the worse the problem became. It was one thing for a child to have such an odd fixation, but then–Robert became a teenager and had a very difficult time relating to his peers due to his pre-occupation with breasts. This, in turn, caused him to spend an exorbitant amount of time alone, at the movies, hoping to find a hero with whom he could identify.

After watching many romantic-dramas, there were two actors with whom he felt a certain kinship: Humphrey Bogart, and Karl Malden.

(The problem was in creating situations conducive for him to emulate the daring manliness of his heroes.)

* * *

It was 1993 and prom night in the suburbs, the most highly anticipated night of the year, and an average American family was anxious to meet their daughter/sister's date for the big occasion. There was a knock at the front door, and the daughter's mother answered as her dad and twin brothers stood up for introductions and 'first impressions.'

A large-nosed young lad wearing a white dinner jacket, a black cummerbund, a red bow tie, and sporting rakishly slanted French beret is welcomed inside.

The daughter, looking as wholesome and lovely as an eighteen-year-old can possibly look, and frankly, a bit like Lauren Bacall in her slightly off-the-shoulder gown . . . faced her family. "Everyone, this is Robert."

One-by-one, Robert went down the line. First, he nodded suavely at the mother and appeared to make a nice impression. Next, he greeted the brothers with a firm, manly grip. It was a little awkward, given their similarity in ages, but all-in-all, that too was a success. Finally, young Robert Longpooper shook the father's hand and mumbled something that had a certain Bogartish lisp to it, which also seemed to go fairly well.

Next came the traditional pinning on of the beautiful corsage. The date took the corsage from its box, and everyone commented favorably as to its beauty. He then, with confident maneuvering, managed to get the corsage pinned to the strap of the gown.

The mother smiled and took a picture of the "Norman Rockwell-ishness" of the moment (a Kodak memory to be treasured for life).

But then, without malice aforethought, the young man was compelled to reach down into the gown and take hold of a breast.

And eventually, after a lengthy period of recovery, Robert Longpooper was released from the hospital, able to return to his high school, pick up his diploma, and set off for "adult life."

From there, his obsession with breasts expanded into a more general category of what was eventually diagnosed as– a primitive need for human intimacy.

And, due to his increasing shyness, he had to devise new and inventive ways to 'meet' women.

* * *

In late 1999, on a quiet day at Mount Sinai Hospital, Robert lay on the table of an MRI machine, receiving instructions from a female technician as to what to expect once he slid into the roomy tubular confines of this high-tech apparatus.

Without looking up from the display-screen, she informed him, "Now, what is most important is that you do not move at all once the table slides you into the tube and the process begins. These tests are very expensive, and insurance companies are especially reluctant to sanction an MRI when the object in question does not even show up in x-rays. You're absolutely certain that you swallowed an ancient Hebrew relic?"

Robert responded matter-of-factly, "Yes."

"Could you have already passed it without knowing?"

"I don't think so," he said.

"Okay. Well, we'll just go ahead and get started. And remember, no movement whatsoever."

After the table slid Robert halfway into the tube, the technician began turning dials and flipping switches. And before long, the machine was emitting a soothing hum as the technician attended to the quantity of data being recorded.

All seemed to be going smoothly until Robert suddenly spoke without moving. "Oh, oh."

The technician looked over at him.

"What's the matter?" she asked.

"I have an itch," he said quietly.

The technician jumped up and rushed over to Robert. "Don't move. Whatever you do–do not move."

"I can't help it," he whined. "I'm gonna have to scratch."

"No! You can't! You'll blur the images!"

"I can't help it. It's the worst itch I've ever had!"

"I'll scratch it! Don't you move! Where's the itch?!

Robert paused for a second. "I'm sort of embarrassed to say it."

"Just say it! I'm a trained nurse. It doesn't matter!"

Robert hesitated, and the nurse demanded, "Where's the itch, God damn it!"

"My testicles."

The technician hastily unzipped his pants, reached inside, and began scratching his balls. This procedure seemed to have a soothing effect on Robert. However, this might not have been the best time for him to expand his growing sexual interests . . . "And also my penis."

The technician gave him a look as she pulled her hand out of his pants.

And soon thereafter, two proctologists were seen throwing Robert out the back doors of the hospital.

* * *

Why Robert Longpooper *fudged* his academic records, joined the Peace Corps, and insisted on the most primitive location possible for his 'assignment' was a bit of surprise–even to his parents, as they had never thought of him as a rugged, outdoors type.

And so, in 2001, near a campfire in the deep interior of the Brazilian rain forest–within easy reach of several bare-breasted native women–Robert Longpooper was laid out in a comfortable position, suckling from the breast of the woman stirring a kettle of thick soup.

Even though the soup was soon ready to be served, he appeared to be quite satisfied and disinterested in ending his present activity.

The 'sucklee' nudged his head and grunted a few words. "Soup's ready, you little pervert."

He ignored her and continued suckling. She then took her heavy stirring-stick and whacked him over the head, which immediately got his attention, and Robert released her breast while she ladled out a spoonful of Amazon critter-soup.

Eventually, after a few years, Robert found his situation in the Corps untenable and returned home.

One of the first things Robert did upon returning to America was to get his hair cut at a barbershop, something that wasn't readily available in the Brazilian rain forest. During this process, the barber asked why Robert hadn't had a haircut in such a long while.

Robert dodged the question, "I spent the last few years with the Peace Corps in Brazil, but I left."

The barber probed for more info as he ran the hair-clippers through Robert's long mane. "Why'd you leave . . . and why are there knots all over your head?"

"I fell out of a tree."

"A hundred times?"

CHAPTER FOUR

Margaret Bennington, who still wore her big thick glasses, had spent the last twenty years in the company of many chickens and much chicken shit, which had led to an extreme shift in her personality. And so, on this particular night in 2019, Margaret sat at a campfire, repeatedly slapping a stick into her hand. She had come to a decision.

Nearby was an old trailer, an old battered pickup truck, and a few old chickens. Twinkling stars filled the coal-black sky, and the moon was in full force. There were no other humans for miles around.

She grumbled, more-or-less, to a chicken, and then mumbled what she had been pondering for the past two decades, "I'm gonna find him, and I'm gonna kill him. I'm gonna shoot him through the eyeballs." And it was on this same night that

Margaret finally uttered her first curse words: "And I hope the dirty stinkin' rotten son-of-a-bitchin' bastard rots in hell."

The next morning, Margaret paced about as she honed her plan. She then jumped into her truck, drove to a public phone twenty miles down the highway, and took her first step towards actually finding the man who ruined her life.

She dialed the phone and spoke, "Good afternoon, this is Special Agent Betsy Pincobulishky. (Garbling the sur-name to give her plausible deniability should things deteriorate to the point where she would need to deny, under oath, imperson-ating an F.B.I. agent named Pincobulishikoff, or Pincobul . . . some-thing-or-other.)

"We're doing an analysis on FXN's building security and need to know if you have elevator surveillance tape in addition to your receptionist's sign-in lobby register?"

Margaret listened to the response, then revealed another layer of her wily skills, "So, if I needed to know the identity of someone who entered your elevator on September 7th, 1999, at approximately 11 am, you would have that information? Correct?"

"Yes, ma'am."

Margaret smiled, thrilled that they had kept records from that long ago. "Excellent, could I have you send a copy of that day's surveillance tape and a copy of the page from that day's lobby registry to our headquarters out in Nevada? P.O. box 7777 Paradise Valley, in care of Special Agent Bennington."

She paused while the woman on the other end of the line clarified the information, then replied, "Yes, that is correct–September 7th, 1999."

Just the simple fact that Margaret Bennington had taken the first step on the road to recovery seemed to elevate her spirits enormously. She then made another call: "Hi Mom, it's me. I think I've finally gotten this thing figured out."

From many miles away, Margaret's seventy-year-old mother spoke into the phone, "Oh honey, that's wonderful. I am so happy for you."

Her mother then directed her voice away from the phone and called to her husband, "Henry, Margaret's on the phone. She says she's finally gotten everything all figured out."

Henry worked his way out of a chair, slowly crossed the room, and took the phone. "That's wonderful, honey. What have you decided to do?" He listened to his daughter's plan, then replied, "Well, that's a good start." Henry glanced over at his wife. "Maggie's decided to shoot him through the eyeballs."

Her mother shook her head. Taking back the phone, she offered her opinion, "I don't think that is a very good idea, honey, not after what he did to us. I mean, your dad and I have had a very rough time because of what happened. It hasn't been easy. So, I really think you ought to give a little more thought to what you're gonna do."

Her mother sensed her daughter's reluctance to change her plan, but her mother was determined. "Shooting him between the eyeballs is a good idea. But there must be a better way of resolving this entire matter. I'm not trying to throw a monkey wrench into your plans–I'd just like you to give it a little more thought, that's all. Please, at least consider poison. It's much more painful."

She then handed the phone back to Henry. "Try and look at it from our point of view." he pleaded. "We raised you from birth to be the greatest human to ever set foot on the planet– and what happens? Some pervert screws it all up. Think about it, honey. Your mother and I were about to become the parents of the greatest human to ever set foot on this planet! But no! 'Mr. Tits' had to come along!"

Margaret, who had found the entire conversation quite validating–but unconvincing–said goodbye to her parents and hung up the phone. She was now more certain than ever that the man who had wronged her would soon be shot through the eyeballs. (Poison really wasn't her style.)

A few days later, at the point where two long desolate roads intersected, Margaret's old pickup truck rolled to a stop in front of a rusty old mailbox.

She got out and opened "Agent" Bennington's mailbox, removed the videotape-sized package and an envelope large enough to accommodate an unfolded page from a lobby registry, and then returned to the truck and left.

That same night, Margaret watched the surveillance videotape on her television set. Nearby, a copy of the page from the registry was on the coffee table next to the opened envelope. She had often daydreamed of how she would first present herself on television. The value of "first impressions" was certainly one of the most–if not *the* most–important lesson drummed into her from birth.

Margaret continued to view the video all the way to its conclusion, then vomited. She had just seen a video of the moment that her spectacularly promising life had been effectively "snuffed out." But now, she had Robert Gerald Longpooper's name, and the search for his location was about to begin.

The following morning, she was on the phone again with her parents, telling them what she'd learned. Obviously, they had questions as to the authenticity of her information.

"Yes, I would assume so," Margaret reasoned. "After all, it is very doubtful that anyone in his right mind would actually choose the name Longpooper."

And while Margaret Bennington had now committed her life to finding and killing Robert Longpooper, Robert had now committed his life to serving God.

CHAPTER FIVE

Robert wore a scraggly bathrobe and stood in front of a broken window in the small, concrete building that had formerly served as a shelter for the homeless. Nearby, a large pot of soup was heating up on a hot plate alongside a stack of empty bowls and biscuits as Robert preached to a handful of extremely disadvantaged men.

And thus, the Church of Bob was born: a humble sanctuary for men dispossessed of hearth and home.

With one hand across his heart and another on the shoulder of one of his "disciples," Bob–or "Reverand Longpooper" as he was known amongst his congregation–spoke, "And now my brothers, before we thank the Lord for our evening meal, let us take a silent moment to ask His forgiveness for any of our past indiscretions."

After finishing his brief 'sermon' and serving dinner to the less fortunate, Robert Longpooper was, for lack of a better term, pooped. The inherent rigors of his newfound path administering to the needy required that he take an occasional break from their long, tedious, seemingly never-ending tales of woe and misery.

Hence, Robert was soon sitting in a cocktail lounge on a bar stool, nursing a cheap beer. Before long, a woman walked in and sat down next to him.

The bartender turned to face her. "Good evening. What may I get you tonight?"

She gave him a pleasant smile. "Well, what would you suggest for a woman who has just about given up all hope of ever experiencing male . . . chivalry?"

Both Robert and the bartender absorbed her question before the bartender was moved to comment, "That is an interesting question, miss . . ."

"Arlene . . . Daljean."

"Very nice to meet you, Ms. Daljean," the bartender continued while drying a glass with a rag. "My name is Michael Perry."

"Very nice to meet you, Mr. Perry," she replied, then turned and smiled at Robert.

"And my name is Robert," he said.

"No last name, Robert?"

He hesitated for a moment. Robert had always been a

bit self-conscious about his last name, but tonight, for some reason–not so much. "Longpooper," he answered.

Arlene pronounced the name, then spelled it, "Longpooper? L-O-N-G-P-O-O-P-E-R.?

Robert nodded. "Yes." She then certified the name. "Robert . . . Longpooper."

"Yes."

"Are you sure?"

"Yes."

Arlene turned back to the bartender. "I would like a double vodka martini, please. And I would like to buy Mr. Longpooper a drink."

The bartender nodded. "Very good." Then he left to fix the drinks. And Arlene turned back to Robert.

"So, Robert," she began, "is Longpooper your Christian name?"

He toyed with the coaster in front of him. "Yes, I believe it is."

"And from what part of the world is your bloodline descended?"

Robert thought about it for a second. "Paris."

"So, you are of the French persuasion?"

Robert nodded to the affirmative. "Oui."

"Okay. All right, Mr.–may I call you Bob?"

"Certainly. If saying my name makes you uncomfortable, just call me anything you want."

"It's not that I'm uncomfortable saying your name . . ."

Robert shrugged. "There are many who are."

"Well, I'm not one of them. I do not judge people by the color of their skin, by their religion, by their annual income, nor by the sound of their name. I am, quite proudly, a liberal democrat."

"I've known women that, because of my last name, would not allow me to even touch their breasts."

"I can assure you," Arlene laughed, "I'm not tainted by that sort of bigotry."

The bartender returned with the drinks. Arlene quickly drained hers and then turned to Robert. "Mr. Longpooper, I would like you to touch my breasts."

In a strategic show of amazing self-control, Robert replied, "Are you sure?"

At this point, the bartender was becoming quite interested in this conversation and leaned forward–almost to an intrusive degree.

Arlene fortified her progressive bonafides, "Yes, I am. And I want this to be a lesson to you. Not all members of the human race are spineless cowards, racists, homophobes, or any of those other fanatical zealots."

Alrene then unbuttoned her blouse and pulled down her bra. "There," she said. "Now, touch them to your heart's content."

Robert reached over and took hold of one of her breasts. "Thank you."

* * *

The following day, back at church–and with his faith in humanity restored–Reverend Bob was now sitting at a table with his congregation, ready to eat. He bowed his head in prayer. "Let us pray. Dear Lord, thank you for providing the nourishment for these temporarily unemployed men of good intentions."

Everyone murmured a quick 'something or other' and then began eating. The Reverend soon noticed that one member of his flock could use seconds. "Brother Raymond, I believe you are in need of further sustenance."

Brother Raymond (ninety years old with one leg, one eye, and no teeth) smiled weakly and garbled his thanks as Bob delivered him another bowl of soup and another biscuit.

Then the Reverend opened his wallet, extracted his meager bankroll, and handed it to Raymond. "It's not much, Brother Raymond, but it's all I have. May it help ease your suffering."

The old man wiped a tear from his eye and muttered a heartfelt thank you.

Later, after his "flock" had moved on for the day, the Reverend got down on his knees, and with tears streaming down his cheeks, bared his soul in prayer. "Dear Lord, please help me find someone who understands me. I don't want to always be alone. Please help me to be better than I am now."

However, old habits were not always so easy to break. Though Robert Longpooper had done his best to walk-the-straight-and-narrow, he was only a man—a man with 'foibles.' Yes, foibles, human foibles, and kinks, and a few quirks, and of course . . . an occasional peccadillo . . . which had all been rekindled by an innocent encounter with a random woman at a bar—near his church, in the same general neighborhood as several other tax-free businesses.

Temporarily revitalized, Bob was, by the end of the week, once again smiling and sitting at the dinner table eating with his congregation. On the one hand, Raymond was gone, even though the Rev's flock had doubled in size, but unfortunately, on the other hand, the church's new charter had only provided for 'female sinners' between the ages of twenty and sixty. Also, in an effort to modernize its therapeutic appeal on social networking, the Church of Bob had now become the Church of Dysfunctional Angels, which specialized in the treatment of nymphomania and featured daily biblical breast baptisms.

Also, in keeping with the church's spiritual values, Reverand Bob had written a special prayer that he liked to recite for his congregation during these baptisms: "Dear Holy Spirit, with the symbolic cleansing of this breast, we offer unto thee in the name of Ezekial all that is worthy of salvation with love and righteousness for those who would seek forth unto the Temple of Eternal Sacramentation."

One day, one of the women he had baptized asked about the meaning of his special prayer. To which Reverand Bob responded, "My child, ours is not to wonder why, ours is but to fly, to fly, to fly with an open heart and charitable arms."

The woman nearly fainted; it was as if she had witnessed a miracle, and she immediately began to spread the word of how 'miraculously progressive' the Church of Dysfunctional Angels actually was. And as more and more women began flocking to his church, so too did their donations. Needless to say, it came as a delightful surprise for Reverend Bob to learn of the kind of money actually made by 'specialists.'

Thus, practically overnight, this so-called "perverted little bastard," whose entire life up to this point had been–let us say–a series of bitter-sweet misunderstandings, had found himself the CEO, COO, and principal stockholder in one of the most successful churches in the country.

CHAPTER SIX

Now that Robert Longpooper had found himself buoyed by an unexpected windfall of tax-free wealth, he was beginning to think of himself in a whole new light: a little taller, a little more dynamic, and of course, a little more French with a much smaller nose. He had also decided to institute the correct pronunciation of his 'family name.'

And within months, on New York's upper-east-side, in a richly appointed lobby, an expensively dressed middle-aged woman walked up to a receptionist's desk and identified herself. "Mrs. Richard Worthington," she said. "I have a two o'clock appointment with Dr. Longpupair."

The receptionist glanced at her computer screen then nodded at the woman. "Thank you. I'll let him know you're on your way up."

Inside Dr. Longpupair's office, the surroundings were exquisitely staged, featuring a comfortable chair and a *very* comfortable lounger. The doctor was sitting at his desk wearing a beautifully tailored, double-breasted, navy-blue pin-stripe suit. He was also sporting a rather handsome goatee, which served him well in offsetting the imbalance from his rather large nose.

Mrs. Worthington entered, and Dr. Longpupair rose out of his chair to greet her. "Mrs. Worthington," he said as he tilted forward in a sophisticated sort of way.

She responded in kind. "Dr. Longpupair." He then took off her coat and hung it on a gold-plated ivory knob, as she stretched out on the lounger.

"Now, where were we?" Dr. Longpupair said, glancing down at his notepad.

She inhaled deeply. "I was telling you about my unnatural fear of being raped by a very muscular ape with a slight Austrian accent. And that's when you decided to treat my illness with the double-handed-heart-massage-procedure."

It was also during this period that Dr. Longpupair began taking an interest in the stock market, where–strangely enough for a man who had very little experience in financial matters– he found himself the beneficiary of an astoundingly lucky series of guesses.

There was no denying that Robert Longpupair was on quite a roll.

* * *

As befitting a man of Dr. Longpupair's importance, he was soon residing in a spectacular, stark-white, Palm Beach mansion fronting a vast stretch of pristine ocean-side sand. Without a doubt, Robert Longpupair had settled comfortably into the lifestyle of the filthy rich and insignificantly famous.

As it did every day, Dr. Longpupair's shiny Rolls Royce traveled up the long driveway while his butler positioned himself outside the front door with a lounging jacket draped over his forearm.

Dr. Longpupair arrived, exchanged his suit coat for the lounging jacket, and entered his estate. He then crossed the plush white carpet, sat at the bar, flicked the stereo on, and fixed himself a drink.

Because he could no longer afford to work for five thousand dollars an hour, Dr. Longpupair had given up his church-sanctioned therapeutic-counseling, and now spent his occasional working hours proposing deals and signing contracts from the deck of his magnificent new estate.

He also dropped the "doctor" designation preceding his name, as it seemed a bit confining to his larger aspirations–he wanted a career that might provide more of a creative challenge. At first, he had considered running for the Presidency of the United States as a Populist candidate. Although, based on a quick assessment of this country's recent history, he felt that the position would not end well. Much like that 'other' guy, he didn't know squat about what the job entailed.

No, he wanted "a more stable gig," yet something that would provide him the creative outlet he so desired. Then it hit him–he would become a Hollywood producer!

Consequently, he sold his Palm Beach mansion to a legendary "fashion icon" from the 1960s who immediately had it painted purple with orange stripes.

CHAPTER SEVEN

Mr. Longpupair then moved to Beverly Hills, bought C. B. DeMille's old place, changed his name again for a sexier moniker, started up a production company, hired an assistant producer at a very large salary, and announced his intention to develop six to eight family-oriented films in his first year.

Robert Longpooper, or R. L., as he is now called, is soon observed whizzing through "the Hills" in a sleek Mercedes convertible.

And, as luck would have it, on Robert's first day in town, R. L. Pictures was able to sign Freidrick Herminator for thirty million dollars to play the lead in a high-concept action thriller about the terrorization of Los Angeles by a muscular actor with a slight Austrian accent. And on that same day, he attached Bill Bozman–acclaimed to be the fastest director in town.

Hence, within twenty-four hours, lights, sound, and camera crews are all set up and itching to go as R. L. quickly verbalizes a fascinating story-line as the first cocktail is being ordered.

And, like Eastweed, Bozman is not one of those artsy-fartsy directors who fret over 'script details' such as meaningful dialogue. He is quite comfortable using an abundant amount of sanctimonious bullshit and self-righteous drivel. And he is "ready to roll . . . now!"

Bozman finishes his Bloody Mary, grabs a bull horn, and commands the set: "Freidrick, you've already swung from the penthouse rooftop down onto the balcony of Darlene Gazette, a single woman in her mid-thirties, just getting home from her job as a gossip columnist for the *Hollywood at Large* magazine."

The bull horn gives a screech of feedback, and Bozman continues, "The backstory on Darlene is that she was raped as a young woman and is still suffering because of it. And now it appears that you have come along with the same criminal intentions.

"You wait, hiding on her balcony behind the barbecue, and watch as she enters her apartment, kicks off her shoes, steps out of her skirt, and listens to her phone messages. Then, with her back to you–as she is jotting down the latest gossip–you sneak up on her."

Bozman sits back in his legendary director's chair and indicates. "Okay, let's try one."

Freidrick has a question. Speaking with a slight Austrian accent, he asks, "And dat's when I–"

Bozman returns to his feet. "Yes. But not in a violent way. R. L. insists on a PG rating." He then sits back down in his chair. "Okay, action."

Darlene enters her apartment, kicks off her shoes, steps out of her skirt, and listens to the phone messages as Freidrick sneaks towards her.

The voice on the answering machine is now heard. "Guess which A-list macho star has been spotted in a Malibu eatery dining with a hooker? Let's just say his last name doesn't start with the letter A, B, C, D, E, or F. And why is it that a certain well-known Disney producer can't seem to confine his evening's entertainment to one Mouseketeer at a time?

Could it be that he has some sort of–wink, wink, nudge, nudge–collaboration issues? And who would have ever thought that one of Hollywood's most important mega-agents would need to show his private parts in public places, or should I say his pubic parts in private places."

At this point, Freidrick is within an arm's reach of Darlene and ready to begin the rape. He reaches out, grabs her neck, flings her onto the couch, and is preparing to pounce on her when the director jumps to his feet.

"Cut! Cut! What the heck are you doing?!" he shouts into the megaphone.

Freidrick unflexes. "Vat do you vant me to do?"

"Don't grab her by the neck and fling her onto the couch!"

"You vant me to screw her on da floor?"

"Freidrick! For the love of Mike! Do you have to use that kind of language?!"

Freidrick shrugs. "Vat do you vant me to say?"

"It's a natural act. Call it what decent people call it: 'making love!'"

Freidrick scratches his head. "But I overheard R. L. say dat I'm supposed to throw her down and rape her."

Bozman's face turns beet-red. "Fuck R. L.! I'm the auteur! Me! Not you! Not R. L.! Me! Me! And we're gonna do it exactly as I say! Fuckin' comprende?!"

* * *

One month later, Freidrick, drunk as a skunk, is at home, laid out on a lounger next to his Olympian-sized pool. A copy of *Variety* is close by, ripped in half, and a nearly empty bottle of scotch dangles from his hand. He looked shell-shocked.

In less than three weeks, the film had been shot, edited, scored, publicized, advertised, and opened in four thousand theaters across the country.

R. L. got his PG. However, the movie, for reasons no one could quite put their finger on, nose-dived on its opening weekend–and as Freidrick's friends were eager to point out, "Probably taking Freidrick's career with it."

Freidrick's wife walks out onto the patio with a large plate of raw vegetables sliced up and decoratively arranged. She holds it out to Freidrick. He looks at her, jumps up, and swats the platter of fresh veggies out of her hands and into the pool.

He then screams, "I am goint to kill dat cocksuckink mudafucka! He has ruint my career!"

"Oh, quit acting like a victim," his wife responds before getting onto the diving board and doing a back-flip into the pool.

When she surfaces, Freidrick is more than ready to continue his venting. "He has ruint me!"

She seems unsympathetic. "You could have told R. L. to shove his thirty million and walked off the set. But you didn't, so quit whining about it."

"Okay, fine! I shut up! But I guarantee you if dat cocksuckink muddafucka eva pulls dat shit on me again–I vill beat his ass into a bloody pulp with my own two hands!"

His wife swims to the edge of the pool and climbs out. "That doesn't even make sense."

"Yes, it does!"

"No, it doesn't. It sounds like you want to spank him. It sounds homosexual."

CHAPTER EIGHT

Because Robert Longpooper had changed the pronunciation of his last name, Margaret Bennington's search for him was temporarily at a dead-end, at least until she could revive her passion to shoot him through the eyeballs.

So today, she is going to drive three hundred miles to the nearest theater, hoping that a movie featuring violent action can re-ignite her hatred for Longpooper, and all the other men who abuse women. Coincidently, she actually ends up being one of the few to see R. L's first film.

And oddly enough, she finds Freidrick Herminator's portrayal of a rapist sensitive and sympathetic, and she makes a mental-note to own her personal copy of *The Nutty Rapist* as soon as it becomes available–which, as it turned out, would be the following Tuesday.

At roughly the same time that Margaret is hunting for a pirated-video of the movie, R. L. is sitting at a desk in a large leather swivel chair looking out the window of his fabulous office. A writer waits, ready to 'pitch' his concept.

With money being no obstacle, R. L. is immediately ready to redeem himself by producing 'a blockbuster.' Consequently, he has begun searching madly for a great concept and scheduling as many pitch-meetings as could be squeezed into a day. And after clearing his throat for the umpteenth time, the writer finally gets R. L.'s attention and makes his pitch.

With a confident smile, he says, "*Little Miss Sunshine* meets . . . *Hannibal Lecter.*"

R. L. reacts, "No," then dismisses the writer with a handshake and a smile. He then pushes a button to signal that the next writer may now enter his office. As the exiting-writer passes by the entering-writer, they give each other a threatening snarl.

R. L. indicates for the entering writer to sit down. "Good afternoon, you may begin whenever you're ready."

The writer places his briefcase on the coffee table, removes a laptop computer, and opens the screen. He then positions a small but very sophisticated tape recorder on the table, turns it on, and makes his pitch.

"Just imagine it: *Star Wars* meets *E.T., Harry Potter, Rocky, Jaws, Titanic, Spider-man,* and . . . *The Sound of Music.* I see it as the most dynamic PG film ever made."

"Whaddya call it?"

"*The Ribilldeebobble.*"

R. L. pushes the intercom button connected to his secretary. "See if Katrina Karoli is available to start next Monday for thirty-five million." He turns back to the writer. "How much you want for it?"

The writer pauses for a moment. "Well, actually, there has already been quite a bit of interest in it. But you know, I don't want to get into the middle of a bidding war. I don't believe in doing business that way. That's an agent's way. I think a writer should just ask for exactly how much he honestly thinks his script is worth, then stick to it no matter what, strictly as a matter of principle. And thus–no agent necessary."

R. L. nods. "What's your price?"

The writer answers boldly, "One mil. Not a penny more, not a penny less."

Again R. L. pushes the intercom button. "Cut a check for one million dollars to . . ." He looks over to get the writer's name.

"Nick Carlson."

He repeats the name to his secretary then looks back at the writer. "It was nice meeting you, Mr. Carlson. Just be sure to get the script to me before Monday morning."

The writer places the computer and the tape recorder back into his briefcase, stands up, and heads out. Pausing in the doorway, he turns back to R. L. "Just out of curiosity–what would have been your top bid?"

"Oh, I don't know. Probably a couple million or so more than any of the other bidders."

The intercom buzzes, and the writer, visibly shaken, leaves.

The secretary's voice is heard, "Ms. Karoli says Monday is fine, and she asked about the title."

R. L. smiles. "It's called *The Nutty Ribilldeebobble*. And you can tell her that I'm quite certain it will be her most challenging role yet."

CHAPTER NINE

Back in the desert, Margaret is stretched out at a campfire near her trailer, under a vast sky with a bright moon and stars galore. She is enjoying a cup of coffee and crocheting an afghan.

She is torn between two obsessions: getting back on Robert Longpooper's trail–or crocheting an afghan for Freidrick Herminator. It is a contest for her soul: a battle between sentimental love and unfathomable hatred.

After working on her afghan a bit more, Margaret has just begun to doze off when an old, bald, bearded, toothless man leading a mule limps into the scene and approaches the campfire.

Margaret studies him carefully before speaking. "What do you want?"

He answers, "Not sex."

Her eyes narrow. "What do you want?" she repeats.

He points at the coffee pot. "Coffee."

"I don't have any."

"That's not coffee there in the coffee pot?"

"No, it isn't."

The old man nods. "Okay. Thanks anyway." He turns and heads off, motioning to his mule. "Come along, Pooper."

Margaret stares into the campfire, and considers something before calling out, "You can come back. I just found some coffee."

The old man returns to the campfire and pulls a tin cup from the saddlebags strapped to his mule. "I got my own cup."

Margaret motion towards the pot. "Help yourself. I found some coffee still in the pot there."

He nods. "Thanks."

After he has poured himself a cup and taken his first swig, Margaret speaks, "I'd like to ask you something if you don't mind."

"I don't mind."

"Did you just say, 'Come along Pooper,' or did you just say, 'C'mon, Longpooper'?"

The old man thinks before answering. "No offense– but I have absolutely no idea of what you just attempted to communicate to me." He then pauses briefly. "Are you a little, you know?"

Margaret stares at him. "What?"

He shrugs, "You know."

She squints. "Stupid?"

The old man nods. "Yeah."

"I was a valedictorian at Harvard University! Now, think, did you just say, 'Come along, Pooper,' as if to tell your mule to come along it's time to go?" She then takes a deep breath. "Or, did you just say, 'C'mon, Longpooper,' as though you might have actually named your mule after someone named 'Longpooper'?"

The old man just stares at her until she continues. "Do you possibly know of an actual family named 'Longpooper'?"

The old man takes another swig of his coffee. "Miss, I would like to give you a little advice before I go, but I will only do it– if you ask for it."

"Go ahead."

"Well, if I were you, knowing what I know after eight decades of living, I would either go gradually back into the city and attempt to make a real . . . 'adjustment,' or I would go a lot farther out into the desert and never come back."

Margaret suppresses an urge to punch him in the nose. "But you don't know any family named Longpooper, right?" He ponders her question, and Margaret presses him once again. "Right? You don't, right?"

The man motions for his mule. "The only one I ever knew with that name was a kid, many years ago. Excuse my language, but he was one perverted little son-of-a-bitch." He then shakes his head, as though trying to expel the memory from his brain. "Can you even imagine the traumatic consequences that might result from a senior citizen being sexually abused by a kid? That was the last straw. The missus and I agreed right then and there that city folk were just too God damn weird, so we packed up two mules and moved out into the desert."

"What was the kid's full name?"

"Longpooper. Robert . . . Longpooper.

Margaret isn't exactly surprised to learn that Robert has a history of causing fully functioning members of society to completely lose their marbles and move out into the desert. "And do you happen to know his current address?" she politely inquires.

"He's a psychiatrist, and I know exactly where he is. Why do you ask?"

Margaret lays her afghan down and gets to her feet. "Because I can't kill him until I find him."

The old man takes a moment to consider things before asking, "Can I go with you and help you kill him?"

"No."

"Please."

"No."

The old man stares into his cup of coffee. "If it weren't for him, my wife would still be alive."

"Well, I'm sorry to hear about your wife, but I still can't take you with me."

He swirls his coffee around. "Why?"

"Because you're old. And slow. And besides that, I just don't like being around men in general. I don't trust 'em." She pauses briefly to get a better look at the old guy. "Although, I certainly do understand your strong passion for revenge on the man responsible for your wife's death. Plus, you'd have to board that mule somewhere–that's not inexpensive. You probably don't have money for that, and where would you sleep. You're damn sure not sleeping in the same room with me."

She waits for his reply, but then winces before proceeding, "It has just occurred to me that you might think you have a little leverage here."

The old man nods.

"And at some point here, you might be intending to tell me that unless I take you with me–you will not be giving me the information on Longpooper's location. Is that correct?"

The old man nods again.

Margaret understands the options of her situation. "What exactly are your terms? And by the way, I am bigger than you, I am stronger than you, and I seem to take offense very easily."

CHAPTER TEN

Margaret, looking thoroughly disgusted, sits in the back of an empty freight truck with her back against the wall. The old man, who had told her his name was Woody, reclines on his back with his arms folded across his chest, his eyes are closed. And the mule, which he insisted come along, stands nearby, snoring in his sleep.

The truck rolls along through the Nevada desert.

Through the Rockies.

Through the Midwestern wheat fields.

Through the beautiful North Carolina countryside.

Then it crosses the Brooklyn Bridge and weaves through the heavy yellow cab traffic of mid-Manhattan. And finally, it turns onto 5th Avenue, travels half a block, and stops in a freight delivery parking space. The driver gets out and goes to the back of the truck to roll the door up.

Sunlight shoots into the back of the truck as the door rises, revealing Margaret, who is pressing her fingers against her nose, and is surrounded by large smatterings of mule poop. The moment the stench reaches the driver's nose, he reacts with a violent jerk of his head, and hurriedly yanks the walk-ramp down to the ground. Coughing and gasping for air, Margaret hastens down the ramp while the old man leads the mule out into the semi-fresh air.

The driver, now holding a handkerchief over his nose, slides the ramp back into its slot and turns to Margaret, who is still struggling to recuperate from the crippling odor.

"In addition to your standard freight charge," he says, "it's gonna be an extra $145 because of the mule shit."

Margaret reaches for her wallet. "What's my total?"

"That'll be $1,785."

Grumbling, she starts counting her money. "I could have taken a plane for six hundred." She then turns to the old man. "I don't suppose you have any money?"

He digs into his pocket. "I got what I been saving for a rainy day."

"Give it to me."

The old man hands over a crumpled wad of bills.

She takes it and counts it. "Four dollars? You saved up . . . four dollars for a rainy day? What were you expecting? Six drops?"

"I ain't worked in thirty years."

Margaret doesn't want to hear anymore. She hands $1,785 to the driver and pockets the four dollars. "Maybe you better wait a few minutes, just in case he's not here. We might need another ride somewhere."

"I'll wait as long as you like," the driver informs her. "Thirty-four fifty an hour. Clock's tickin'."

Margaret beckons the old man over for some confidential, last-minute instructions. "You still got that hammer I gave you?"

The old man pulls the hammer from the mule's saddlebags.

"Okay. Now, Woody, you stand over there by the door." Margaret indicates to the big revolving door under the sign reading: *Mental Health Clinic–Specializing in the Latest Techniques of Framodorickian Counseling*. Then she points to the hammer. "If you see him running through the door trying to escape, hit him in the head."

Woody nods, and Margaret enters the building, heading for the lobby's receptionist's desk.

Woody calls to her, "I haven't seen him in over thirty years. What's he look like?"

Unfortunately, Margaret has already passed through the doors and is unable to hear his question. She approaches the receptionist. "Good afternoon. Could you give me Dr. Longpooper's suite number, please?"

The woman on the other side of the counter lifts her head up from her computer monitor and responds, "I'm sorry, could you give me that name again, please?"

"Longpooper. Dr. Robert."

The receptionist seems puzzled. "Longpooper?"

Margaret nods. "Yes."

"I'm sorry, I'm not familiar with the name. Let me ask my supervisor." She presses a button and speaks into the intercom, "Hi, this is Elaine, can you tell me if you are familiar with one of our doctors, a Longpooper?"

The voice of her supervisor comes back, "Well, if I'm not mistaken, I'd have to say you are probably talking about Dr. Sven Svensenborg, the Swedish specialist in left-handed masturbation therapy. As a matter of fact, just last week, I was talking to Svenie, and he told me that he was thinking of changing diets because he can't seem to get his weight below three hundred pounds. So, if you're a three hundred pound man, you've naturally gotta be a long pooper, wouldncha think?"

Margaret and the receptionist exchange looks of confusion before Margaret satisfies their mutual needs. "Don't even bother trying."

The receptionist chuckles. "You know, I do remember there used to be a doctor here with a name that sort of sounds like Longpooper. His name was Longpupair."

"What did Dr. Longpupair specialize in?" Margaret asks.

"Breast-fondulation therapy."

"And do you know where Dr. Longpupair is currently practicing?"

The receptionist ponders for a moment. "The last I heard, he'd hit it big in the stock market and retired to an oceanside mansion in Palm Beach, Florida."

Suddenly, the front entrance explodes with shouting and scuffling. Margaret turns around to see Woody in the revolving door, chasing a uniformed US mail carrier around, hammer in hand.

"That's not him! That's not him!" she screams.

Minutes later, Margaret, Woody, and the mule are once again in the freight truck en route to somewhere. Margaret now seems a little more sympathetic to the old man's feelings. "So, what was it that caused your wife's actual death?"

Woody sighs, noticeably haunted by the memory. "The missus was having one of her frequent nightmares, and when she woke up to get a drink of water, she slipped on a pile of Pooper's poop and sat on a big fat spider who gave her a fatal bite on the butt."

Margaret faints. Woody fans her face with his dirty old handkerchief. She soon revives. "What happened?"

Woody puts his handkerchief back into his pocket. "I was telling you about my wife's nightmares, of constantly being molested by a French Cub Scout with a big nose."

Margaret faints again.

The truck rattles through the Carolina's under a full moon.

* * *

Meanwhile, back in Brooklyn, at the old Longpooper residence, Frank and Angela are now in their early sixties.

On this particular night, Frank is watching Monday Night Football in the living room, and Angela is busy in the kitchen preparing dinner. The crucifix still hangs on the wall, next to a cheap reproduction of a famous Renaissance painting depicting baby Jesus suckling at the breast of the Virgin Mary.

"Frank?" Angela asks from the kitchen. "What do you suppose that old guy, Mr. Woody, wanted to talk to Bobbie about?"

With his attention still primarily focused on the football game, Frank shrugs. "I dunno."

"How do you suppose he got our phone number?"

"I dunno. Probably looked in the phone book."

"Frank?"

Frank waits for a commercial, then cranks his neck away from the TV and toward the kitchen. "Yeah?"

"Were you surprised when Bobbie first told us that he was a psychiatrist in New York City?"

"Yeah, I guess I was. Outta all the kids, I just always figured he was the dumbest. I never did expect him to amount to nothing."

Angela nods. "I just hope he's finally outgrown that weird problem of his."

CHAPTER ELEVEN

With the aid of a microphone, an assistant herds a group of Hollywood hopefuls into the R. L. Pictures studio. Spread across an entire side of a soundstage, a mural of *The Nutty Rapist* is still proudly displayed.

"Okay, listen up," the assistant instructs. "This is the casting line for Baron Von Trapp's oldest-daughter role*, only*. If you are here for any other role, you are in the wrong line."

A couple of guys dressed as cowboys leave, a couple don't.

"Now, be absolutely certain that your current phone number is on all your 'headshots.' If we can't reach you by phone, we cannot cast you. Also, as you can see, there is a long line today, so your audition will be brief.

"You'll meet R. L., he'll give you an 'interactive-palm-reading' based on cinematic-method-projection, and then a call-back list of thirty girls will be posted on Monday. So, don't be nervous, just be yourself, and good luck to each of you."

A few steps down the hallway from the front of the line, R. L. sits on a heavily cushioned bar stool in the center of a very impressive office. The heads of many African animals hang on all the surrounding walls. He has a small microphone clipped to the lapel of his nifty-looking safari jacket. His assistant producer, Edward Turwilliger, sits nearby with a clipboard and a pencil.

At this point, it is probably noteworthy to mention that R. L. has spent twenty million dollars to hire Edward Turwilliger as his assistant for one reason: Edward has a legendary reputation as the only Hollywood producer who has never lost money on any movie that he has ever been associated with. And it is considered a great honor and privilege to be the recipient of his meticulous planning and incomparable insights to guarantee the successful outcome of any project he agrees to put his name on.

R. L. speaks into his lapel, "Next."

A gorgeous twenty-five-year-old enters the room and walks up to R. L. She smiles while unbuttoning her blouse. "Good morning."

"How are you?" R. L. asks.

"Fine, and yourself?"

"Fine, thank you."

The girl rolls her shoulders back, and R. L. reaches out and takes hold of her breasts, fondles them in a variety of ways, tucks them back into her blouse, and smiles at the girl as he directs himself to Edward. "Nine-point-three."

The girl pouts her lips.

R. L. generously offers an 'upgrade,' "Make that a nine-four."

Edward notes the change on his clipboard as the grateful starlet curtsies and–after placing her 'headshots' atop the large stack already on R. L.'s desk–leaves, smiling.

Once outside, the gorgeous girl is greeted by her friend, and they head off, discussing today's audition.

"How did it go?" the friend asks.

"I think it went really well," the gorgeous girl replies, adding, "I think we interacted in a very visceral sort of way."

"What did you get?

"A nine-four," she answers proudly.

Her friend gives her a fist-bump. "I looked the line over pretty carefully. I think a nine-four definitely gets you on the call-back list. I don't think a nine-three is gonna make it. But I think nine-four is pretty much a lock."

The gorgeous girl nods in agreement, "That's how I had it figured. I'm jazzed. The best my old breasts ever did was a nine-one."

CHAPTER TWELVE

Margaret, Woody, and the mule are still in the back of the freight truck, traveling across the Eastern Seaboard. The two human occupants pass the time in conversation.

"Margaret," Woody asks, "what are on those videotapes that you carry around?"

"One's called *The Nutty Rapist*. And the other one . . . isn't."

"What are they about?"

Margeret lets out a deep, empathetic sigh. "One's about a heartbreaking journey through the lonely world of sexual alienation."

"What's the other one about?"

"The sick perversion of a sex freak."

Woody has a confused look. "Is that what's called a porno movie?"

"No."

Woody scowls. "I wasn't brought up to watch filthy movies."

Margaret shakes her head. "These aren't filthy movies."

"My parents, God bless their souls," Woody responds, visibly shaken by their memory. "They'd roll over in their graves if they knew I was on a first-name basis with someone who watches dirty movies."

Margaret slams a fist against the truck bed, narrowly missing a fresh pile of mule excrement. "They aren't dirty movies!"

Woody backs off. "Guess I'll just have to take your word for it."

"When we get to Florida, I'll play one for you, and you can see for yourself. Now quit bugging me," she mutters before turning away from him.

After rolling along a coastal highway for a lengthy period of increasing stench, the truck finally stops at a roadside phone booth. The driver gets out and rolls up the back end of the truck. Margaret staggers out, coughing and gasping for air. (Woody appears to be okay with the smell.)

The driver holds his nose as he looks inside at the latest piles of mule poop. "This one is also gonna cost you another $145 on top of the standard freight charge."

Margaret enters the booth and searches for an address in the phonebook. Then, still choking from the whole stinking ordeal, she returns to the truck and directs the driver. "9272 Oceanside Drive."

Within the hour, they arrive at the front entrance gates of their destination. Once again, the driver unlocks and rolls up the rear door, and once again, the passengers disembark. Margaret is in a particularly foul mood and is not overly polite in dealing with the business at hand.

"What's my bill?" she snaps.

"It's $1,525 for the haul. Plus $145 for the mule shit. Plus another $145 for the additional mule shit."

Margaret opens her wallet and snarls at Woody as she counts out the money. "I don't suppose you came into any money these past few days?"

Woody shakes his head. "Nope."

Margaret hands over the last of her money, and, for both Woody and the driver's benefit, shakes out the now empty wallet.

The driver slides the money into his wallet. "The meter's running if you want me to wait."

"No need to wait," Margaret answers, "and I'd just like to say thank you for getting us here safely. And thanks in particular, for not violating that very excellent law which bans the opening of any door whenever a freight vehicle is moving."

The driver nods at her. "You are very welcome. And I wish you both the very best. And Pooper too."

Woody waves. "Thanks for the ride."

The driver climbs back into the truck, and just like that, he's gone, leaving only fresh air in his absence.

Margret grunts at Woody. "And so, the lousy rotten son-of-a-bitch who ruined both our lives . . . is now within two hundred yards of us."

"What's the plan?" Woody asks while gently petting Pooper, who seems to be a bit antsy from such a long trip. Margret rubs her hands diabolically.

They wait for darkness to fall, allowing Margaret to sneak from palm tree to palm tree, as she heads for the mansion. Woody is close behind. And, cognizant of losing the element of surprise, Pooper–and his latest pile of poop–has been left tied to a tree, downwind.

They continue to sneak from tree to tree, quickly approaching the mansion, which has its lights off. However, Margaret could still get a sense of its majesty, and it made her blood boil. She couldn't wait to *do him in*. They cautiously circle around the mansion, and, with the ocean at their back, approach it from the beach-side. Once there, they crouch at the foot of the stairs leading up to the marble patio encircling the pool.

Margret's heart is racing. "So far, so good."

Woody is heartened by her assessment. "Everything's going good, right?"

"Perfectly."

Just then, Pooper brays loudly, breaking into the stillness of the night.

Margaret is startled back into Woody, and his arms are involuntarily flung forward around her chest in an effort to keep from tumbling over backward as her arms are flung wide open–one straight up over Woody's head and the other straight down into his crotch.

Woody's got her by the tits.

She's got Woody by the pecker.

Their grips tighten as they struggle to keep from hitting the ground.

After they've regained their balance, Margaret silently threatens Pooper with her fist. She then glances at Woody and grumbles, "It's okay. It wasn't your fault." And again, she threatens the mule with a silent fist. "I knew that stupid mule was gonna cause trouble."

Woody puts a finger to his lips and softly hushes Pooper.

Margaret speaks quietly, "Okay, Woody–it's time. On the count of three, we rush him."

Woody isn't quite ready. "Don't forget about our guns."

Margaret shakes her head. "I decided against guns. We're gonna kill him with our bare hands."

"We're not gonna shoot him through the eyeballs?"

"Bare hands," she clarifies.

"You gonna take Longpooper?"

She responds with a nod.

"Who do I take?"

"Longpooper."

Woody hesitates for a moment. "We both take Longpooper?"

Margret answers with a smile, "Yeah."

Woody thinks for a second. "What do you think we should do if there's anybody in there with him?"

"Ignore them. I don't want any innocent bystanders hurt. No matter what."

Woody scratches his head. "We'll just go in there and kill him with our bare hands, and then what?"

"That's all."

Woody continues scratching. "No getaway plan?"

"I don't see how that would be possible."

Woody wonders out loud, "Life without parole."

Margaret gives him a look.

Woody doesn't want to appear cowardly. "Okay. I guess it'll be worth it. Although I gotta tell ya, I think I've still got about ten or twelve pretty good years left in me."

Margaret understands. "Yeah, that's the shame of the whole thing. You've got another ten or twelve years, and I've probably got another forty or fifty. That's a lot of years we'll be giving up."

This was, in fact, the first time since Margaret made the decision to shoot Longpooper in the eyeballs, that she had put much thought into her life beyond that point.

Woody breaks the momentary silence. "Maybe it would be better if we didn't kill him. Maybe we ought to just beat the living shit out of him."

"Yeah, good idea. I never was quite comfortable with the thought of being a murderer. And besides that, if we don't kill him, then we could come back and beat the shit out of him every year. Okay, that's the plan, on three. One, two, three."

And off they go.

Seconds later, Margaret and Woody stand in a living room with moonlight flooding in through the oceanside glass wall. They assess the situation.

"Maybe he's at the movies?" Woody suggests.

"No, it's too late for the movies. He's probably gone for the weekend. We'll have to wait for him to come back."

"I hope he left some food," Woody replies, scanning the kitchen area.

Several hours pass. They have made themselves comfortable. Margaret sits next to the pool, feeling tamed by the black starry sky and the gently rolling ocean. Inside, Woody lays back on the couch with his feet up, watching television, eating a sandwich, and drinking a beer. The mule has taken to grazing in its general vicinity.

Another hour passes before Margaret stands up and heads off toward the beach. From his comfortable position on the couch, Woody calls to her. "Margaret, I thought you were gonna show me that sex movie that isn't a porno film."

Margaret pauses to respond, "It's in my coat pocket. Go ahead and play it if you want."

She then crosses the marble patio, descends the stairs, and walks off to the clean white beach, with each step pressing her foot into the deep sand. She is soon relaxing into her moonlight walk until something suddenly occurs to her. She pivots and races back through the deep sand, heading for the mansion.

(Unfortunately, it is impossible to actually race through deep sand. And the harder one tries, the worse it gets . . . until one finally stumbles, sprawling face-first onto the beach.)

At least that's how it went for Margaret, three times.

With spasmodic determination, she eventually reaches the mansion, dashes up the stairs and across the patio, and into the living room. The blank television screen hisses softly in the darkness. Margaret looks at Woody, and with his jaw dropped open and a stunned look on his face, Woody stares at the hissing television.

"Woody," she sputters, "there were two videos in my coat pocket. One is in technicolor, and the other one is in black and white. Which one did you happen to watch?"

Woody can barely mumble a response, "The other one."

Margret approaches the couch. "So, now you know why I hate him so much."

Woody looks guilty.

Margaret sympathizes. "It's okay–it wasn't your fault, you didn't mean to watch it. Besides, you're eighty years old."

Woody remains silent for a few seconds before asking, "Margaret, can I show you why my wife nicknamed me Woody?"

Margaret takes a step back. "Woody! Get a grip!"

"Sorry. It's just that on the video there, your naked flesh looked so darn–"

"Woody!" Margaret shouts at the top of her lungs.

Woody reacts sheepishly, "Sorry."

She vigorously admonishes him, "You're eighty friggin' years old!"

"Sorry."

"Act your age, you horny old pervert!"

"Sorry."

* * *

A few miles away, a doctor, a nurse, a lawyer, a daughter, and Mr. Wilburn, a one-hundred-year-old billionaire, converse as they are being chauffeured back to Mr. Wilburn's purple mansion. "We hope for the best," the lawyer says to Mr. Wilburn, "but we prepare for the worst. And given all the time and effort that we've put into keeping your will current, it is my belief that you are as well prepared to pass along the Wilburn Estate, as it is possible to be."

"Thank you, Arthur," Mr. Wilburn responds before turning to the doctor. "Palmer?"

"You're doing okay," the doctor answers. "Your heart rate is strong. Your cholesterol's good. And most importantly, your blood pressure is not too bad. It could be better. But it's okay. You're holding steady."

"What is the single most important thing I can do to stay alive?" the billionaire asks.

"I'd say you should avoid any situation in which your heart might suffer a sudden shock."

Moments later, they arrive at the mansion. Mr. Wilburn, being as old as he is, takes his time to disembark from the vehicle. In the meantime, the lawyer walks inside. He doesn't think much about the fact that the lights are on. But then the lawyer's eyes fall upon Margaret, Woody, and a mule, each looking like a deer caught in the headlights.

While the lawyer is still processing the particulars of this scene–especially the mule–the doctor, the nurse, the daughter, and Mr. Wilburn enter the house. And they too, are suddenly caught up in the bizarre possibilities of the moment.

Before any questions are asked, the lawyer yells as he races out the door. "It's the Manson family!"

The nurse and the doctor are right on his heels.

Consequently, only the daughter is left to catch the decrepit old body falling backward, dead as a doornail. She cradles her father in her arms, wailing loudly in deep sobs of grief.

Margaret turns her head slowly to Woody and whispers, "I don't think this man is Robert Longpooper." But just to be sure, she approaches the body for a closer look, causing the daughter to scream, "Murderers! Murderers! Murderers!"

CHAPTER THIRTEEN

A month after the death of Mr. Wilburn, R. L. is laying back on a lounger next to a therapist. "I don't know what's wrong with me," he says despondently. "I should be happy, but I'm not. I'm depressed."

The psychiatrist writes something down on her notepad. "Specifically, what is making you so depressed?"

"I can't find a good script."

"I've heard the buzz on *The Nutty Ribilldeebobble* is pretty good," she says sympathetically.

R. L. sighs. "It'll open. But for my new one, what I'm really looking for is something a little more character-driven. Something based on passion and revenge, yet steeped in irony. I want to pull a small human-life story out of the back pages of a newspaper and give it grandeur and meaning."

The psychiatrist thinks for a moment. "I recently read something that I thought might make an interesting movie."

"What was it?" R. L. asks.

"Well, my parents still live in Florida, Palm Beach, and they send me their local newspaper just so I can stay abreast of what's going on back home. And a few days ago, there was an article about some old guy who keeled over from a heart attack when he returned to his home and came upon a couple of burglars waiting for him."

"Go on," R. L. says, rising up from the lounger.

"And so, the D.A. is prosecuting the burglars for murder, and he's asking for the death penalty. However, they claim they had only gone to the house to visit an old friend."

Immediately, R. L. can feel his creative juices flowing. He smiles at the psychiatrist. "Excuse me. I have a phone call to make." He quickly dials a number, and a few seconds later is heard giving instructions, "Edward, R. L. here. There are two burglars in Palm Beach, Florida, who are on trial and may get the death penalty for causing a fatal heart attack. Buy me the rights to that story as quickly as possible. Whatever it costs." R. L. hangs up and lays back down.

"Is the inability to find a good script all that is depressing you?" the psychiatrist asks, getting back into the subject of his session.

R. L. thinks for a moment. "No, I guess not. The truth is that I feel unfulfilled. Unworthy. And, kind of guilty."

She understands, "That is a very common neurosis amongst people who have acquired sudden, unexpected, and enormous wealth. The psychiatric term is low self-esteem."

"What should I do about it?" R. L. asks, staring at the ceiling.

"You need a complete makeover. Top to bottom. Including name, hairstyle, wardrobe, make of car, and of course–the ol' schnozzola. Might even wanna' tweeze the brows."

CHAPTER FOURTEEN

It had only taken Edward about ten minutes to secure the rights to the incident down in Florida, and he is now waiting for instructions as to how R. L. wants to proceed with the project.

Just then, Turwilliger's phone rings. It's R. L. "Edward, listen, I just came up with something enormous. I want to run it past you. For our next picture, *The Nutty Burglars*, I want to cast amateurs–real people from real walks of life. I don't want the fancy wine crowd. I want coffee drinkers. Whaddya think, yes or hell yes?"

Edward hesitates for a moment. "Well, actually, wouldn't real actors be better? Especially for, like, you know . . . dialogue?"

R. L. ignores the question. "By the way, you never told me how you like my new name or my new hairstyle. Yes, or, oh yes?"

"Oh yes. Totally. Definite improvement on both."

R. L. probes, "And the brows?"

"Exquisite."

"And my new leisure suits to go with my matching Land Rover?"

"Very sexy."

R. L. is satisfied. "Okay. Get busy on my 'real people' idea. Bring me some hidden camera footage, and I'll choose the ones I want. By the way, how do you like my new . . . you know?"

"Major improvement. Huge. Definitely worth whatever extra you had to pay."

"Do I remind you of Bogie?"

"Like two peas out of the same pod."

A call-waiting signal beeps, and R. L. responds, "Got another call, gotta go." Edward can hear him pick up the other line. "Roland Valtrain speaking." Then Edward's line clicks off.

It is a nice name; Edward had to give him that.

Later, amongst the Beverly Hills Starbucks crowd, two slick, young dressers sit at a table, sipping coffee. One of them notices the pocket dictionary that the other has placed on the table. (Behind them, a man with a camera inconspicuously videos various patrons.)

"You still gettin' into that dictionary every day?" the first slick dresser asks.

The second dresser nods. "You've got to talk the talk if you want to move upstairs where the real money gets split up. It's all about how you communicate. And especially, it's all about your vocabulary."

At another table, two agents talk business. One of them throws his hands up. "The guy is an absolute total pain in the ass, idiot. He wants me to get him the lead in a musical-comedy because he has finally learned how to lip-sync and play the air-guitar."

At another table, two actors discuss roles. "So, what do you think of that slimeball getting the new *Bond* role?" the first one gripes to the second.

"Total phony. Hair-plugs and heel-lifts," he responds. "*Entertainment Magazine* called him 'The rugged stud from down-under.' Shit. He's about as rugged as my sister."

The first actor laughs. "He ain't no Roland Valtrain, that's for damn sure."

On the other side of the room, two producers talk about their next project. "That new Carlson script is brilliant. Best script I've ever read," the first one declares.

"I agree," the second says, nodding. "It was perfect. Let's option it, fire Carlson, and bring in the guy who did the *Ribilldeebobble* rewrite."

"He's expensive. Maybe we ought to just stick with Carlson?"

"No way. He's too old. Christ, the guy has got to be in his mid-twenties. We need somebody more in touch with a younger demographic."

At another table, two successful writers talk.

The first one stirs his coffee. "It's only a one-scene-dialogue-rewrite, but I'd like to make enough to at least buy myself a new Mercedes."

"Well, you're the best dialogue writer in town, make 'em pay through the nose. So, specifically, what's wrong with your old Mercedes?"

"Ah, you know, that fuckin' fucker's all fucked up."

Two actors converse at another table. "How was your audition this morning?" the first one asks.

The second sighs. "They hated me. Director's a total asshole."

"I think part of your problem might be that you're sort of defensive, and maybe even a little paranoid."

"No, I'm not! You're just saying that because I'm getting bald!"

At another table, a young macho actor is being interviewed for a magazine profile. "How do you feel about the tremendous success of your first movie?" the interviewer asks.

With crossed arms, the macho actor replies, "As far as I'm concerned, Hollywood can kiss my ass while I'm farting."

The interviewer smiles and writes down his comment. "I'll quote you on that."

"Yeah, and here's another one you can quote me on: I rode into this town on my motorcycle with eighty-seven cents in my pocket and the t-shirt on my back. And I can leave the same way. So, Hollywood can kiss my ass while I'm fartin'."

"You already said that last part," the interviewer reminds him.

"Okay then, change that last part. Say that I said, 'Hollywood can kiss my ass where the sun don't shine.'"

"That's a little redundant, isn't it?"

The macho actor strokes his chin. "Okay then, do that part about the motorcycle, the twenty-seven cents, and the t-shirt, and then say–"

"I think you said eighty-seven cents, not twenty-seven–"

"Whatever. Then say I said . . ."

Two actresses sit at another table. One speaks, "You'll never guess who I saw last night at the supermarket. Mertle Street. What a lovely person she is."

The other one gives her a look. "What were you expecting? Some foul-mouthed bitch with nipple rings?"

* * *

In Roland's pied-a-terre penthouse, Roland and Edward are watching a videotape of the Starbucks hidden videotape footage. The tape recording starts with the two slick dressers. As they stand up to leave, the *second one* picks up his dictionary from the table and puts it into his pocket, and indicates to his friend as they walk out past the smiling face on a large Republican campaign poster. "Ya know, that shit-wad is one abysmally odious motherfucker, ain't he?"

The videotape soon finishes, and Edward clicks off the television and turns to Roland, "What do you think?"

Roland beams with enthusiasm, "I like it. Real people. Salt of the earth. Naturalness. Authenticity. That's what I'm talking about."

"Roland, I have to say it . . . you are a visionary."

Roland responds, "Hang on–it's gonna be a very bumpy night because I just had another bolt of brain-lightning. This is gonna' blow your socks off." Roland takes a deep breath and continues, "Listen to this: For *The Nutty Burglars*, we cast the real burglars . . . as themselves."

Edward considers the realities of this brilliant revelation. "We're gonna have criminals star in the movie?"

"That's what I'm thinkin'."

Edward clasps his hands to better process his thoughts. "But, aren't these people going to be behind bars on death row, and . . . unavailable?"

Roland shrugs. "We'll have to get them acquitted." He then thinks for a second and continues, "Hire Johnny Cottran. Stack the deck. We need somebody clever enough to play the race card."

"I think Johnny's dead," Edward responds.

"Okay. Then hire somebody else just like him–a smooth talker. Snappy dresser. A brilliant legal mind. Someone who is above reproach and inspires the confidence, respect, and admiration of his fellow colleagues."

Edward thinks for a moment. "Bill Bart okay?"

"Don't be ridiculous."

"Sorry."

* * *

A few weeks later, Margaret and Woody are seated in a courtroom waiting for a verdict. Their attorney, Bruce Butler, is a barrel-chested man with a shaved head, wearing a black fedora and a top coat. He has just given his closing statement to the all-white jury of six old, toothless, bearded guys and six pissed-off-looking cowgirls who are approximately Margaret's age.

"If not now," Bruce begs passionately, "when? If not you . . . who?" He hands two pairs of child-sized shoes to Margaret and Woody, and continues, "If the shoes don't fit . . . you must acquit."

CHAPTER FIFTEEN

Bruce stands in a motorhome sales office, negotiating for the sale of a super-sized *Winnebago*. The salesman, Carl, is anxious to accommodate. Woody still can't believe how well the trial had gone and that he isn't going to spend his last days behind bars. Margaret is a little more resistant to the way things are going.

"Carl, let me ask you this," Bruce says, stroking the potential of a very tasty financial windfall possibly coming his way. "If I give you cash for the biggest, finest, most expensive motorhome you have, can you, today, right now, deliver it?"

Carl salivates at the prospects of his gigantic commission, putting him in a very, very agreeable state. "Yes, I can–yes, sir. I can have it ready to roll off this lot in five minutes. Less than five minutes. Three minutes."

"Excellent," Bruce replies, reaching out to shake the man's hand. He then turns to Margaret. "Now, are you and Woody ready to drive your new motorhome to Hollywood and star in a movie as soon as I hand each of you five thousand dollars?"

Margaret smiles sympathetically to convey her appreciation for all that Bruce has done for her and Woody. "I'm sorry. It's a very nice offer, but Woody and I are already committed to . . . doing something else. Right, Woody?"

"Well, yes, but," Woody begins, before turning to Carl and Bruce, "could you fellas excuse us for just a moment?"

"But–" Carl begins, sensing a disaster about to happen to his sale.

Bruce skillfully intercedes, "Yes, of course, by all means." He then guides the visibly shaken Carl to the door. "Come along, Carl. Let these fine folks have a little privacy while they discuss their luxurious new lifestyle." As he passes through the doorway, Bruce looks back. "Did I fail to mention that the five thousand cash dollars is in addition to the one million cash dollars that you will each receive for the Tasmanian rights to your story, along with the other one million dollars that you will each receive for starring in *The Nutty Burglars*, which begins shooting next Monday morning?"

Woody glances at Margaret, then back at Bruce. "We each get five thousand dollars cash, plus one million more dollars cash, plus another million dollars cash, each, both of us?"

Bruce nods, with a disarmingly friendly smile. "Precisely. Aside from my sixty percent commission."

With Bruce and Carl finally out of the room, Woody and Margaret can have their private time for considering the matter.

Margaret leans against Carl's desk, pauses for thought, then speaks, "It's a very nice offer, but I think we should really stay focused on what we're doing."

"What are we doing?" Woody asks part rhetorically and part because it is hard to think about much else with all the money that is currently staring him in the face.

"We're gonna catch the man that ruined both our lives–and beat the living shit out of him with our bare hands!"

"But–"

"Woody! We're gonna find Longpooper, and we're gonna get our revenge on the dirty, slimy perverted stinkin' little weasel that was responsible for killing your wife and ruining my career."

"Okay. You're right. I'm sorry. I just had a weak moment thinking about us being broke and homeless. But you're right– we have to stay focused."

* * *

It isn't long before a big, luxurious Winnebago is traveling down the highway. Margaret is at the wheel, Woody is hiding somewhere in the back, and Pooper is standing in the kitchen, looking rather comfortable in his new pad. Still keeping her eyes fixed on the road, Margaret speaks over her shoulder. "I think we did the right thing, Woody. We'll finish the stupid movie and then get right back on Longpooper's trail. And in the meanwhile, we'll have enough money to hire a detective to track him down for us."

Margaret stretches out her shoulder muscles and continues with their plan, "Then we can just go get him without wasting a lot of time having to find him. I really think we did the right thing. Don't you agree? Woody?"

Woody doesn't respond, and Margaret knows why. She pulls the Winnebago off to the side of the road and stomps back to the bedroom, where she pounds on the door, startling Woody, who is, just as Margaret assumed, masturbating.

"Woody!" she shouts through the closed door.

"What?" he shouts back.

"You're playing with yourself!

"No, I'm not."

She attempts to twist the locked doorknob. "You give me that video right now!"

"I don't have it."

"Yes, you do! And I want you to open this door and hand it out right this second!"

"Can you come in and get it?"

Margaret smacks the door with her palm. "Woody! You're being disgusting!"

"I'm sorry."

She hears him shuffle around a bit before handing the video through the narrowly opened door.

Later, Margaret pulls the Winnebago into a rest stop for the night. After a bit of tossing and turning, she eventually finds a comfortable position on the cramped couch where she attempts to catch a little shut-eye, but Woody, who is sitting at the kitchen table depressed, is eating his beans as obnoxiously as possible. Pooper is outside, tied to a trash bin that is bolted to the ground.

Eventually, Woody finishes his beans and asks, "Margaret?"

She refuses to open her eyes. "What?"

"Can I watch your video tonight?"

"No," she answers, sternly.

"Please."

"No."

Woody sighs and remains silent for nearly a full minute. "I'll give you a million dollars."

"Woody, geez, c'mon. Can't you live out the rest of your life like one of those decent old guys who just sit around and stay out of the way?"

"Margaret, can I be honest with you?"

Margret grunts. "If you must."

"I need a piece of ass."

"Woody! Knock it off!"

He starts crying.

81

Margaret feels the pangs of compassion. She gets up from the couch, puts her arm over Woody's shoulder, and offers him some words of comfort: "Woody, please don't cry. Things are not as bad as they seem right at the moment. At the moment, you are just vulnerable and feeling the loss of your wife, and the deep empty void that followed her death after the wonderful relationship you two shared for so many, many years.

"You're feeling sad and lonely, and you yearn, hopelessly, for just one more day, just one more hour, just one more minute, with that irreplaceable woman, your partner in sickness and in health, for better or for worse, until death did you part.

"You're grief-stricken with a broken heart, languishing in the gloom and despair of knowing there is no possible hope for her return . . . that's all that's wrong with you, Woody."

Woody's quiet crying breaks into gulping sobs, and Margaret holds him tighter until he can convey his innermost feelings. "I just wanna fuck sumthin'."

Margaret removes her arm from his shoulder and gives him a look of disgust.

Defeated, Woody plods back into the bedroom, and shortly thereafter, is heard in a peaceful snore.

Now that a second wind had been practically forced upon her, Margaret spends some time on the couch reading. Eventually, she puts down her book, stretches, goes over to the closet, takes the technicolor video from her coat pocket, puts it in the VCR, and returns to the couch to watch it.

On the television screen, the video begins to play, starting with the bold title for *The Nutty Rapist.* Margaret immediately fast-forwards to the PG-rated rape scene:

Freidrick swings down from a penthouse rooftop and lands on Darlene Gazette's balcony. He hides behind the outdoor barbecue and watches as Darlene enters her apartment, kicks off her shoes, steps out of her skirt, and listens to her phone messages while taking notes.

Then, with Darlene's back to him, Freidrick sneaks quietly towards her as the answering machine begins playing: "Guess which A-list macho star has been spotted in a Malibu eatery dining with . . ."

At this point, Margaret fast-forwards through most of the message and slows it back to normal speed just after Freidrick has reached Darlene and is about to attack.

". . . or should I say his pubic parts in private places," the answering machine says.

Freidrick reaches for Darlene. "Darlene."

She is startled and screams. Wide-eyed in fear, she faces him.

He continues, "Do not fear, my precious. For as pitiful and undeservink as I may appear to you . . . it is only your blessink dat I seek.

"I seek it today, I seek it tomorrow, ant I seek it forever, for it is more glorious to me dan da heavens above us.

"You haff been wrongt by a stranger. And I am here today to plech to you my sacred vow of obedience.

"And to giff you my word of honor dat I shall fine da one who has violatet you, ant return him to you . . . for your revench.

"Ant now, under da mighty gaze of Aphrodite, da Goddess off Love, let us unite as one, dat I may receef your blessink for my mission."

Freidrick lifts Darlene up into his arms and, brushing a single tear from her cheek, carries her into the bedroom.

And the scene now slowly dissolves into ocean waves crashing onto the shoreline, as *The William Tell Overture* is heard building into the action, with Freidrick and Darlene entwined in a passionate embrace.

Margaret pauses the tape with heavy tears pouring from her eyes.

The following morning, the Winnebago whizzes past a sign that reads: TEXAS STATE LINE. Half-asleep, Woody cracks open his bedroom door and whines, "Do you have to drive so fast?"

CHAPTER SIXTEEN

Poolside at his fabulous mansion, Roland Valtrain relaxes on a lounger, reading the script for *The Nutty Burglars*. And due to the extent of his marvelous new landscaping, the upper half of his body–including his marvelous new face–is hidden from view.

He puts the script down and makes a call to Edward.

"Roland Valtrain's office, Edward Turwilliger speaking."

"Edward, Roland here. Are you sitting down?"

"Yes."

"Okay. Listen to this. And boy are you going to be glad your future is in my hands. I have just, less than ten seconds ago, decided . . . to direct *The Nutty Burglars* myself."

There is no immediate response, and Roland continues, "Well, what do you think? Is there now hope for all mankind or what?"

"We're not going to have a . . . regular director?"

"Can't trust this baby with anyone but myself," he answers, then continues, "Okay, here's what I want you to do. Fire the writer, bring in somebody with a more 'ooh la la' sensibility, make it a Frenchman. And get the new draft over to me by six o'clock. Comprende?"

Edward, who is starting "to-lose-it," responds, "You want a European to write a new script by six o'clock?"

"If he can have it by five, that would be even better. And tell him to change the location to France; I want accents." He pauses for a moment, pondering another brilliant new idea for the movie.

"And make the Margaret Bennington character sixty years older, and the Woody Johnson character sixty years younger. I want the younger-man older-woman dynamic.

"We're going to make a critically acclaimed art film, Edward. And I don't give a damn about the box office. Valtrain Studios is going to be known for quality, not crass commercialism. Au revoir."

With that established, Roland hangs up.

Edward opens his desk drawer, extracts a container of pills, swallows two, puts the cap back on the container, returns the pills to the drawer, quickly re-evaluates matters, re-opens the drawer, re-opens the container, and swallows two more pills.

* * *

86

Meanwhile, as the Winnebago cruises through San Diego, Woody is still feeling grumpy, "Do you have to play the radio so loud?"

* * *

Roland is still tanning by the pool in the privacy of his beautifully landscaped new gardens. And still, he can only be seen from the shoulders down. He is daydreaming about his Oscar speech.

His inner voice speaks, "First, I'd like to thank the Academy for this year's Best Director award. It is a privilege and an honor . . . just to have been nominated in the same category as a Hitchcock, a Fellini, an Altman, a Spielberg–any of the three Brooks, or, you know, Sturges, Wilder, that whole gang."

He pauses to evaluate his speech before expressing his concerns: "I dunno," he mumbles to himself. "It seems to lack a certain . . . sincerity. But . . . I suppose I could fake that part."

Roland comes out of his daydream to make a call.

Edward answers, "Roland Valtrain's office."

"Edward, you sitting down?"

"No."

"Sit down. I'll wait."

After a brief pause, Edward says, "Okay, I'm sitting. What happened?"

"Listen carefully. You are about to hear evolution at work. Are you ready?"

"I guess I am."

"Hire Larry Lavere . . . to be my assistant director."

"Oh my God."

"Offer him sixteen million dollars and keep going up until he says, 'okay.' Au revoir."

Edward sits back in the big swivel-chair, leisurely takes off one shoe, then one sock. Then, in a very athletic way, he reaches his toes out and grips the desk drawer-handle, pulls the drawer open, and gives the drawer a calculated kick from below–which sends the container of pills flying up into his waiting hands. Whereupon, he opens the container, takes out a pill, flips it into the air, and catches it in his mouth.

He then takes out another pill, situates it on his thumbnail, flips it into the air, and positions his mouth for the catch.

Back at the pool, and still only visible from the shoulders down, Roland enjoys his afternoon of sunbathing–as his inner voice slips back into his Oscar speech daydream to set-up a punch-line to precede his exit from the stage.

"And finally, let me just say that I would like to dedicate this Oscar to Bob Hope and all the women I have ever had a relationship with, however brief or one-sided it may have been."

Roland now mulls over the punchline to further extend his 'Oscar knowledge.' "Then, as I turn to leave, I wink and say, "thanks for the mammaries." But he immediately realizes the obvious weakness of that choice. "Nah. Clever, but, way too corny."

Then Roland makes another call.

"Roland Valtrain's office," Edward garbles.

"Me again. Let me run a quick one by ya. You ready?"

"Let 'er roll."

"Video documentary. Title: *Breasts*. You've got half the world interested in the subject matter at all times. Correct? Gotta open huge, right?"

"Youuu got it," Edward slurs, "You're rall over thish one, Roland."

"But . . . problem. No time. I've got the *Burglars* shoot starting Monday. And then there'll be the New York awards. And then I'll have the Oscars, and there's the festival at Cannes. When am I gonna have time to do a documentary that'll probably eat up at least five years just shooting raw footage? An absolute can't-miss-foolproof-concept, but it's got to go back-burner. File the concept in my things-to-do-later box. And stay tuned. Au revoir."

Edward remains seated in Roland's office, balancing a plastic spoon on the edge of his desk. He then places a pill in the spoon, positions himself just right, and pounds his fist onto the stem of the spoon–which sends the pill shooting up into his open mouth.

Back on the lounger beside the pool, Roland is still only observable from the shoulders down as his inner voice continues to refine his Oscar speech.

"I want to thank the Academy for honoring me with this award. I didn't think I'd win, so I didn't prepare a speech. However, I would just like to say that it has been a long, winding, and bittersweet road that has taken me from one modest little breast in Brooklyn–to this gathering of the world's brightest stars in celebration of this year's most outstanding breasts. Thank you, and God bless America."

Roland pauses to reflect on what he has just said. Then, murmurs to himself, "Nah. Too obvious. Not enough subtext."

He pulls himself out of his daydream and turns towards the mansion. "Angelina!" he shouts.

Shortly thereafter, a gorgeous Italian woman walks from the living room through the open glass doors and out onto the poolside patio where Roland's face remains obscured by a large hanging-pot of geraniums.

"You called?" she asks.

His voice filters back through the geraniums, "I think I'd like my lunch now."

"What would you like?"

"Two tomatoes, two carrots, one turnip, six radishes, a glass of water, and a small piece of chocolate."

"Sounds yummy," she coos before turning to leave.

"Angelina?"

She turns back. "Yes?"

"How much am I paying you?"

"One million."

"For how long?"

"One week."

"And what are the actual terms of our contract? Can you recall? I've forgotten."

"You give me one million American dollars, and I come over to your house and fix your lunch every day for one week."

"Okay. Thank you."

Angela leaves to prepare Roland's lunch, while his inner voice brings a financial matter casually to his attention: "A million dollars. Geez. I gotta start cutting back on unnecessary expenses."

Roland makes another call and Edward answers. His voice sounds a bit more slurred than when last heard. "Yo, Valtrain's offish."

"It's me. Quick thought before I forget. French location . . . unnecessary expense. Change it to Florida. But keep the accents. Fire the French writer, hire a Floridian. Au revoir."

Edward gulps down another pill, turns up the volume on Jerry Lee, reaches into the desk drawer, and pulls out a bottle of tequila.

Back at the pool, Roland is heard drawing in a deep breath from his excitable new nostrils as he absorbs the fragrance from his marvelous new gardens.

A few minutes later, Angelina brings out his lunch and sets it on a nearby table, blows him a kiss, and, flashing her most sensual smile, waves goodbye. "Ciao. See you tomorrow."

Roland has something on his mind and begins the process of revealing it. "Angelina?"

"Si?"

"Do you suppose there is any possible circumstance under which I might be allowed to snuzzle either one or both of your breasts . . . with my nose?'

Angelina hesitates momentarily, then answers, "No, I don't think so."

"No chance at all?"

She crosses her arms. "I guess I could ask Antonio."

"How soon could you get back to me?"

"How soon do you need to know?"

"Very soon," he answers.

"Well, I guess I could ask Antonio now; he's out in the limousine waiting for me."

"That would be great."

"Okay. I'll be right back," she says before turning away.

Roland returns to the exaggerated sounds of sniffing his flowers, and in between sniffs, he's able to scribble out a check.

Angelina returns with bad news. "Antonio says absolutely not under any possible circumstances."

Roland holds the check above the flowers for her to see. "I'd be willing to give you this check for five million dollars."

Angelina glances about, then takes the check and tucks it into her bra. "Just one."

A short while later, Antonio and Angelina are in the limousine, swaying through Beverly Hills on their way home. Antonio is gradually growing angrier and angrier over Roland's outrageous pass at his wife until he is eventually moved to threaten to avenge her honor. "I should go back and beat that man to death for what he say to you!"

Angelina is willing to overlook Roland's affront to her morals. "Let him live, my darling. He has a mental sickness."

Her words seem to appease Antonio, at least temporarily. "However, my darling, I was thinking, this man who is so sick, I just wonder if he could be cured, if he were able to actually . . . snuzzle your breasts, just one. And I was thinking, what would the cure for such a humiliating sickness be worth in American dollars–before the tabloids learn of this disgusting perversion."

Angelina is appalled. "Antonio!"

"I make a joke with you, my darling–you know that. I just make a joke with you. Come, kiss me, my darling. Tell me you know I was just make a joke."

Angelina slides over to him.

"My Antonio, who would kill before allowing another man to even think such thoughts. Kiss me, my darling."

Antonio notices something inside her bra and picks it out. "What is this?"

Angelina shrugs. "It is nothing."

Antonio looks it over. "It is a check for five million dollars."

Angelina shrugs again. "I cannot remember where it came from."

"Maybe you found it on the beach or somewhere?"

"Yes, now I remember; I found it on the beach. Kiss me, my darling, and make love to me."

"Now, in the limo?"

"Yes, now, in the limo, on the way to the bank."

* * *

Back at Roland's gardens, from behind an exquisite display of roses, Roland makes another call.

Edward answers, in a happy warble, "Yeah, yeah, and yo."

"Edward, quick reminder. Meeting. Florida location. Monday morning. Cast and crew. All actors in full makeup and ready to start shooting. Au revoir."

CHAPTER SEVENTEEN

The Winnebago arrives at Valtrain Studios, where a five-story high movie poster for *The Nutty Ribilldeebobble* still adorns the side of a soundstage.

It depicts Katrina Karoli as "Maria," singing to Darth Vadar in the Alps, as other members of the Von Trapp family, including the nine-point-four starlet, dance with E.T., Harry Potter, Rocky, and Spider-man, while a great white shark lurks below the surface of Lake Geneva where many attractive survivors cling to floating debris from the sinking Titanic.

A security guard at the entrance gate stops the RV to check Margaret and Woody's credentials.

He peruses the inside of the Winnebago without seeming to notice Pooper, then asks, "May I have your name and the name of the party with whom you have an appointment?"

Margaret answers, "Margaret Bennington and Woody Johnson. We were told there would be someone here waiting for us."

The guard checks his list, then adjusts his attitude. "Yes, of course. Good afternoon, Ms. Bennington, Mr. Johnson. Just pull straight ahead and park in any of the reserved spaces. You'll enter building C and take the elevator to Mr. Valtrain's penthouse office, where Mr. Valtrain's assistant producer Edward Turwilliger is expecting you."

They park and enter the building and head for the elevator. After a short ride, the penthouse elevator doors open, and they step out and approach the receptionist's desk. Margaret speaks, "Margaret Bennington and Woody Johnson to see Edward Turwilliger."

The receptionist is very congenial. "You may go right in. Mr. Turwilliger is expecting you. And welcome to Hollywood.

"I think you'll be extremely happy working with Mr. Turwilliger, whose personal conduct exemplifies the absolute highest standards of professionalism while always staunchly defining his legendary commitment to the art of classic movie-making."

Margaret smiles. "Thank you."

Then, she and Woody approach the great oak doors to meet this legendary Hollywood icon.

They enter and freeze in their footsteps, reacting to what they see: Mr. Turwilliger, minus shoes, socks, and shirt, is engaged in an arm-flapping, leg-wobbling dance, with his mouth hanging open and his eyes fixated on the ceiling fan, as Jerry Lee shrieks, "Goodness! Gracious! Great balls of fire!"

The following morning, a passenger jet crosses the sky with Margaret and Woody on board, heading to Florida for the filming of *The Nutty Burglars*. Their voices are heard coming from within.

"I don't know why the hell we couldn't have just stayed in Florida and waited for 'em," Woody grumbles.

"Quit complaining. We'll do the movie, get our money, I'll have Lasik surgery on my eyes, and we'll go beat the crap out of Longpooper. Everything's gonna be fine. So quit griping will ya, geezuz."

"I miss Pooper. My teeth hurt."

"Woody, I've had a bellyful of your bullshit! Now shut the fuck up!"

CHAPTER EIGHTEEN

As the sun breaks slowly over the horizon, the cast and crew are gathered outside the walls of the mansion where the actual "crime" depicted in *The Nutty Burglars* took place. They are waiting patiently for Roland Valtrain to step out of his trailer.

Margaret, now wearing a gray-haired wig and granny glasses, is made up to look ninety years old. And in an attempt to make Woody look sixty years younger, he is wearing a LeBron James tank-top and has barbed-wire tattoos circling his sagging, eighty-year-old biceps. His new hair is spiked blond, and his new set of teeth appear to be a little too big and a little too white.

At this point, Roland, script in hand, steps out of his trailer, revealing his face to the general public for the first time since his total makeover. He is almost unrecognizable without his huge nose. It's like a ten-pound pink potato in the center of his face–has disappeared.

He even looks a little like Humphrey Bogart. Slightly. (It is probably because he is dressed in a white dinner jacket identical to the one Bogie wore in *Casablanca*.)

He is in a joyous mood and ready to get started. "Bonjour, bonjour."

The cast and crew return a hesitant chorus of "bonjours."

Roland turns to Margaret and Woody. "May I take just a moment before we start to welcome our stars, Mademoiselle Bennington and Monsieur Johnson." A brief applause follows before Roland continues, "Today, my friends, we are about to embark on a great journey, a journey that will take us into the deepest recesses of artistic possibilities–if we allow it.

"If we make ourselves 'available' as artists . . . then by the almighty grace of God, we shall succeed.

"And thus it is–that I have chosen to shoot this film in the great tradition of . . . Monsieur Cassavetes." He pauses briefly to let the weight of his words sink in. He then continues, "This film shall be shot . . . without a script."

Roland then tears the script apart and cavalierly throws it off into the balmy breeze. "And now . . . let us begin! Monsieur Johnson, tell me, where were you standing on the morning of that fateful night?"

Woody points. "I was over there, and then I was over there for a while, and then I was–"

Roland interrupts, "And where were you just before you actually approached the house?"

"I dunno. I guess I was over there someplace."

"Very good. You go stand over there someplace. And mademoiselle, will you please go stand where you were standing."

Woody and Margaret go stand by the mansion's entrance gate as Roland turns to the cameraman and points at the purple mansion. "I used to have a white one just like that."

Roland then walks over and huddles with his two actors. "Now, Woody, tell me about that day."

"Well, as close as I remember, Margaret said that the lousy rotten son-of-a-bitch who ruined our lives was only a couple hundred yards away, and–"

Margaret interrupts Woody with a chuckle and a nudge. "What Mr. Johnson means is that–in reference to the man who had just robbed us and was running off with all our hard-earned money–I said, 'the-son-of-a-gun is already two hundred yards away . . . and so . . . we probably wouldn't be able to catch him.'"

Roland nods his understanding. "Ah oui, so there was a crime, and you, who were actually the innocent victims, were soon thereafter to be falsely accused of committing an even more unspeakable crime . . . the murder of Monsieur Wilburn."

"Yes." Margaret nods in complete agreement.

"Injustice. Injustice. Now I think I am beginning to understand the motivation behind mademoiselle's anger."

Roland turns to Woody. "All right, now, let me ask you this: Were you fearful that the criminal might return and kill mademoiselle?"

Woody shakes his head. "Not that I can recall."

Roland persists, "But what if he had returned, and what if he had shot mademoiselle, and what if–unbeknownst to you– mademoiselle was not quite mortally wounded, but had merely taken a few slugs in her butt, what might you have said as she lay in your arms, gasping for breath?"

Woody thinks before answering. "Goodbye."

"Would you have said 'goodbye,' or would you have said something more like, 'We'll always have Paris'?"

"Nah, I wouldn't have said that–I've never even been to Paris."

Margaret nudges him again.

"Oh yeah, I forgot about that time I was in Paris during the French war."

"So, with a strong but gentle, seductive but sincere, lusty but noble look on your face. . . . you would have said, 'We'll always have Paris'?"

"Yes."

Roland claps his hands together and heads for the director's chair, loudly instructing as he goes. "Quiet on the set, please! Everybody, in position! Let's try one!" But first, he pauses to check through a French pocket dictionary. "Margaret, instead of saying 'that son-of-a-gun,' could you say, 'that son-of-a-canon'? Canon means gun in French."

"That son-of-a-canon?" she echoes.

"Eef yu dond mine," Roland says in an exaggerated French accent, "aye leetell mur nayzell, pleece. Mur lak zis, 'Zat-son-off-eh-kaynon.'"

* * *

Later, after the first day's filming had finished, Margaret and Woody are spread out on a couple of blankets on the beach near a campfire. Woody is laid back with his hands behind his head, and Margaret is sitting with her legs crossed.

"You know," Margaret says, thinking aloud, "there's something about that guy, Valtrain."

Woody turns onto his side to face her. "Margaret, I'm sorry to have to tell you, but as soon as this movie's finished, you and me are splitting up."

"You're not going with me to beat the shit out of Longpooper?"

"Nope. Now that I've got enough money to get inside during the bad weather, and buy a little food and medicine, I've got some hope for the future." He rolls back onto his back and stares up at the sky. "And I don't wanna spoil my future messing with any of that violence bullshit. Pardon my language."

"Where will you be going?"

"Don't know exactly, but I'll probably end up somewhere–hang-gliding in the nude."

Margaret closes her eyes and shakes her head. "Woody, Woody, Woody. Sometimes, when I think of you, I just think to myself, 'Oh, Woody, Woody, Woody.'"

Times passes as the waves lap onto the shore, lulling them into a peaceful slumber. Margaret is warm and comfortable between her blankets. Woody appears to also be asleep–until one eye opens. Then the other. He then crawls around the campfire, takes off his clothes, and slides in between Margaret's blankets.

Before long, a soft moan escapes from Margaret's dream. "Freidrick."

Her dream then morphs into the scene where Freidrick 'rapes' Darlene, but with Woody in the Freidrick role. As the ocean waves crash onto the shoreline, *The William Tell Overture* builds the tension, and the sounds Margaret is making grows gradually louder and louder. "Freidrick! Oh, Freidrick!"

In the morning, the cast and crew gather together, waiting for Roland to step out of his trailer and give them their direction. Woody and Margaret stand off to the side of Roland's trailer. She has her arms crossed and is angrily tapping her toe. "Woody," she begins, "I want you to tell me exactly what you meant by that last remark."

Woody has his head hung low. "I'm sorry if it made you feel bad. I don't want you to feel bad. You know that."

Her foot-tapping continues. "No, I don't know that. I thought we were getting along rather well."

"We get along fine. It's not that. It's just the age thing, that's all."

"So, you're seriously telling me that I'm not old enough for you?"

"Nothing personal. You're a very nice young lady. But you know, some women around your age start getting a little bossy, and they generally stay that way until they lose their hearing." He shrugs. "And so, you know, at this point in my life, I'd kind of like to find me an old deaf chick."

"Are you saying I'm a bitch?"

Woody looks up at her. "Well, you know, sometimes you do get a little bossy."

"I get bossy?"

"Well, ya know, sometimes."

"Well then, do you know what you get sometimes? Let me tell you what you get. You get a little . . . wise-assie."

Woody lowers his head again. "Yeah, I know I'm not exactly perfect myself. But I'm sure you know that I do like you a lot. Even more than a lot."

Right on cue, Roland Valtrain, still in a white dinner jacket, steps out of his trailer and greets his cast and crew. "Bonjour, all you wonderful people. Today we will shoot the final scene of the movie."

Roland's assistant director, Larry Lavere, eventually asks the question that appears to be on everyone's tongue. "Today, we're shooting the last scene of the movie?"

Roland nods. "Oui."

"But what about suspense and plot twists and things like that?"

Roland scratched his chin. "Well, I guess I could throw in a little twist there at the end–like they did in *Chinatown*. Maybe Margaret could turn out to be the old man's daughter or sister or something like that?"

Lavere looks totally discombobulated. "We're shooting a two-day movie?"

"Oui, oui. Tomorrow we start the editing. I'll cut-in an hour or so of *Eiffel Tower-Moulin Rouge* stuff. Thursday, we throw on a fabulous score. And Friday, we'll be in theaters in time to qualify for the Oscar nominations. And that, my friends, is when we reap the harvest of all our hard work."

A worried-looking member of the camera crew interjects himself into the conversation. "This movie is a two-day paycheck?"

Roland walks over and claps the crew member on the shoulder. "Every fabulous one of you will be paid double the usual salary that you would receive for a regular full-length shooting schedule." Then, he throws in a little Frenchness to soften their apprehension, "How does zat suit you?"

Everyone cheers except Lavere, who hesitantly inquires, "I don't suppose that double salary thing would include me, would it?"

"Lar," Roland says, turning to face him, "I think I've got you locked in at sixteen million, don't I?"

"Yes, I believe that was the figure we settled on."

"I'll tell you what, even though we're bringing in this movie way under budget–I've still, just for professional reasons, I've still got to hold you to your original contract." He clears his throat and continues, using his best impression of a charming French accent as he remembers it from the Pepe Le Pew cartoons. "Howevair, I weel throw in a nize leetle bonez. How does zat sound to you?"

Lavere gives Roland two thumbs up.

* * *

That evening, in an airport parking lot, Woody (once again bald and toothless) and Margaret are saying their good-byes.

Woody, with a small duffle bag of possessions, looks lovingly at Margaret, "If you ever get back out to Nevada, I'll be there, some-place close to where I first met you. Me and Pooper will probably have a real comfy little trailer up in one of them gulches."

Margaret smiles lovingly at Woody. "I sure am gonna miss you, Woody."

He smiles back at her. "And I sure am gonna miss you." Then he smiles again and winks. "And so is Woody."

Margaret lovingly slaps the top of Woody's head. "Woody, you stop that right now. You nasty old thing."

He laughs. "Okay, you gorgeous creature, I'll save it for the next time I see ya."

CHAPTER NINETEEN

The following week, Margaret, who has recently undergone Lasik surgery and now looks quite different without her large glasses, pokes her head into Valtrain's office to say goodbye before leaving to start her new life. Valtrain has taken to wearing a white dinner jacket and a beret as his daily attire, and presently sits in the big swivel chair with his feet up on the desk, reading the latest edition of *Variety*.

"Hi." Margaret smiles. "I just wanted to stop by before I leave to wish you good luck with your Oscar nomination."

Roland stands up and invites her in. "Gee, you look so . . . different without your old gray wig and your glasses. I'd never even recognize you. Entree, entree. We shall have a farewell toast."

Margaret enters somewhat reluctantly as Roland goes to

the wine chiller, pulls out a bottle of champagne, twists out the cork, pours out an initial taste into two very elegant flutes. He hands one to Margaret and makes a toast. "Here's to you, kid."

They each take a long sip and savor the fine quality.

"Challon-sur-Marne, 1947," Roland says.

Margaret protests coquettishly. "Oh, Roland, you shouldn't have."

"Nothing is too good for the star of *The Nutty Burglars*."

"Oh, Roland, don't be silly," she demurs.

"And nothing . . . is too good . . . for the soon-to-be . . . Academy Award nominee . . . for Best Actress of the Year."

"Oh, Roland. Quit that. I'm just a girl that lives in a trailer out in the desert. Besides, why would you even think I'd be nominated."

He shrugs. "I should have told you before, but I just assumed that you knew."

"Knew what?"

"That you were brilliant."

Margaret gushes, then indicates that she might not object to a slight refill. "Perhaps just a drop."

Roland refills both flutes and makes another toast. "To the brilliantly sophisticated . . . and thoroughly charming . . . winner, of this year's *Oscar*, for Best Actress in a motion picture . . . Ms. Margaret Bennington."

"Oh Roland, you just quit that. Gosh almighty, you know I'm

not going to win," Margaret modestly adds with a smile before draining her flute.

Roland then drains his, takes hers, and refills both. However, in reaching for her refill, Margaret reveals a slight tipsiness in her demeanor as she bumps her fingertips against the flute, spilling a full measure of champagne onto Roland Valtrain's pants–from his belly button to his crotch.

Margaret appears horrified by what she has done. "Oh my gosh! Do you have any water?!"

Roland indicates to the open bottle of Evian on his desk as he sits onto the desk's front lip. She grabs the bottle, gets down on one knee, and pours it carefully onto Roland's crotch, vigorously brushing out the champagne stain with her fingers.

"I am so sorry," she says.

Roland doesn't seem quite as troubled by the incident. "No problem."

"I don't think champagne stains, but if it does, I'm sure this water will get it out." Margaret finishes smoothing out the wrinkles in his pants, then stands and shrugs as she sets the half-empty bottle of Evian back on the desk. "I think I got it all. I did my best."

"Maybe you should open my zipper to circulate some air down there so my pants will dry out."

"Good idea," she agrees. Margaret then pulls down his zipper and fluffs his pants–a procedure that registers prominently on his face.

Roland refills Margaret's empty flute and raises his to make another toast, but first, he makes an innocent suggestion: "Margaret, why don't you take your coat off and get comfortable?"

Margaret removes her coat and flings it onto the arm of the couch, causing a videotape to fall from its pocket. Margaret picks up the tape and puts it back into her coat pocket. "I really shouldn't stay–I really should go."

"Let me toast to not only the greatest living actress of our time . . . but also to a wonderful woman with delightfully wholesome moral values."

Margaret smiles, sips twice, and is ready for another refill. Roland accommodates, and as he hands her the refill, it is, once again, bumped by her careless fingertips.

Roland reacts swiftly and is able to catch the falling wave of champagne with his crotch–through the open zipper.

"Oh my gosh," Margaret gasps. "What's the matter with me?!" She grabs the water bottle and begins the same process as before: soak, rub, soak, rub.

"Sacra blue!" Roland exclaims in his most Le Pew-ish French. "At last! I haff found zee woman who understands me! C'est moi! C'est moi! I haff found zee luf uf my life! Marry me, marry me! But first zee stain mon cheri, zee stain!"

CHAPTER TWENTY

Time has passed, things have happened, and Margaret has adapted surprisingly easily into Roland's 'country-club' lifestyle, and they have never been happier. At the moment, they both have their heads under the covers of their bed at the Valtrain estate.

Apparently, buoyed by the elegance of his new nose, Roland has decided to go full-nasal French. "Oh my leetle coookeee, you are so beeyooteefull. I luff you! I cannot leef weeze out you! You muss marry me, you muss!"

"I love you too, Roland, but–"

"But what, mon cheri?"

Margaret is reticent to re-visit the subject, "You know. I've told you."

"Zee man in zee video tape?"

"Yes."

"You muss haff revenge? Why my leetle flowair?" Roland must have this thing settled. "Why?"

"Because he's a pervert," she says flatly, without emotion.

"But mon ami, su am I. And you luff me."

"Yes, but you are different. He is a filthy pervert. You are just a man who passionately appreciates the true beauty of the female anatomy. Believe me, you two are nothing alike."

"Sank you, my leetle pudding. But I muss insist zat you forget zat pervert. I will keel him for you! And zen we shall be married!"

"Let me think about it."

"You may sink about eet one more day. But tomorrow night, after zee Academy Awards, you muss show me zee videotape, and zen I shall see who is zeese man I must keel to avenge zee honor off my leetle cocquette." Roland pauses for a moment. "Now, take my toe, and put eet . . ."

In the morning, Margaret and Roland go for a swim in the pool. The good night's rest and the clear perspective it has brought to this day's needs has jogged Roland's memory. "Woody called yesterday to wish you good luck tonight, and had a suggestion for your Oscar speech."

"What did he say?"

"You can listen to his message. Eet is on the answering machine."

CHAPTER TWENTY-ONE

Oscar night has finally arrived and is well underway. The host, Spencer Hobson, is at the podium to introduce the final nominee and show a clip from her movie.

"And now, the final nominee for Best Actress, Margaret Bennington, for her role as Francoise Dubois in . . . *The Nutty Burglars*."

The lights dim, the curtains part, and on a gigantic screen, the final scene from *The Nutty Burglars* begins to play.

A number of people that were originally seen in the candid video footage taken at Starbucks are playing the roles of Mr. Wilburn, the doctor, the nurse, the lawyer, and the French police officers.

In the Wilburn mansion, as French sirens signal the arrival of the police, Margaret cradles the one-hundred-year-old man in her arms. He is dying bravely, and she is sobbing profusely.

It goes on and on, until finally, the old man gathers his last bit of strength, looks up at the very old looking Francoise Dubois, and utters his final words: "Francoise Dubois . . . au revoir . . . mama."

He then coughs a couple of times, and croaks.

But Francoise's sobbing continues, until finally, Woody, hair-spiked and tank-topped, swaggers into the scene, embraces Francoise with his barbed-wired biceps, and, after overcoming some mild protesting, is able to pull Francoise away from her dead son and guide her off into the foggy night.

As she's pulled away, a few bullet holes are noticed in the derriere region of Francoise's Ingrid-Bergman attire.

The clip ends, the orchestra music starts up, the lights grow brighter, and a beautiful presenter opens the envelope. "And the winner is . . . Margaret Bennington for *The Nutty Burglars!*"

Margaret throws her hands over her mouth at the shock of winning. She stands, kisses Roland (who still wears a white dinner jacket and a beret), and heads for the podium. Once there, she is handed her Oscar.

At which point, she gives a most heartfelt acceptance speech. Looking out at the audience, she smiles. "Thank you so much. This is a dream come true. I truly did not expect to win, so I didn't prepare a speech. But I would just like to take this most glorious moment of my life to only say one thing, and that is . . ." She pauses and takes a deep breath.

"I agree with my friend Woody, who just tonight left a message on my answering machine, saying that it is now time for the human species to have a single gene scientifically eliminated from its DNA–the one that makes possible the human capacity for violence."

She then waits patiently for the uproar of applause to subside. "And, I almost forgot to thank my mom and dad, the two greatest parents in the world! And John Brown, my golf instructor. And Roland Valtrain, who made the whole thing possible." Margaret then waves and walks off the stage.

It is soon time for the rollicking Oscar after-parties to get underway.

The night's tension has been released, and the parties are just starting to get sloppy, as a sleek, black limousine drives up to the front entrance of a famous Beverly Hills restaurant, where an excited crowd mills about with autograph books, cameras, and microphones in hand.

The doorman opens the limousine door, Roland steps out, waves to the crowd, then offers his hand to Margaret. And then, along with her Oscar, Margaret steps out, carrying a large, black, rhinestone beach bag. The crowd cheers with love and adoration.

Another doorman opens the restaurant doors, and they enter, where a very star-studded Hollywood crowd has gathered to cap off the night in style. Then, a hostess escorts them to their front-and-center-reserved-table to join the other winners.

Roland speaks confidentially to Margaret, "No matter what time we get home tonight, no matter what kind of shape we are in, you weel still play me your video, oui?"

"Oui," Margaret responds.

After they reach their table, many hugs and kisses are exchanged. They sit. Champagne is poured. The world is perfect when Charles Karstens, Hollywood's Handsomest actor, approaches Roland. "When I heard you were not nominated for Best Director, I almost quit the Guild in protest," he confides.

Roland gives him a sincere smile. "Thank you."

"And then I thought to myself," Charles continues, "*The Godfather* meets *One Hundred and One Dalmations*."

Roland considers it for a moment, then responds, "No."

Disappointed, Charles leaves.

A very large handsome man now approaches Roland, shakes his hand, gives him a pat on the shoulder, and speaks solemnly, "I vas soo sorry to hear aboud Edvard."

Roland temporarily discontinues his French accent. "Yes, he was a lovely man, but what can one do?"

"Yes. Drucks. A shame. A damn shame."

"Personally, I think it would take more than just drugs to cause a person to actually believe that he is an ostrich . . . and can fly off of a four-story building."

"Vut do you sink caust it?"

Roland shrugs. "Haven't got a clue."

"Led me ask you somesink. Vut do you sink of zis: *The Herminator* meets *Mr. Smith Goes to Vashington*?"

Roland considers the question. "No."

The large handsome man stomps away, pissed, brushing away Margaret's attempt to hand him the hand-crocheted afghan that she has pulled out of her beach bag.

A popular movie star approaches. She and Roland exchange air kisses. "Picture this," she says, "*Joan of Arc* meets *Catherine the Great*?"

Roland pictures it. "No."

The star turns to make her exit. "Well, if you ever come to your senses, gimme a call; I might answer."

After a few hours, as the crowd starts to thin out, Roland listens to one last pitch:

"*Ishtar* meets *Hudson Hawke*?" an elderly studio-executive asks.

"Sounds interesting–call me tomorrow."

CHAPTER TWENTY-TWO

Roland and Margaret arrive home at four a.m. As they enter the doors of the estate, Margaret has her shoes in one hand and her Oscar in the other. Roland is drunk and happy and ready to speak a little French.

"And now, my leetle humming bird, before I hum for you a niiz song, let us watch zee video so zat I can see zee man who I must keel before I can be married to my leetle angel of sweet, sweet, souffles. Oui?"

Margaret smiles. "That was my promise, oui?"

"Oui, oui, ya, ya."

"Then you shall have it," Margaret confirms as she walks into the bedroom.

Roland fixes them a drink and sits on the couch in front of the television. Margaret returns, video in hand. She inserts it into the VCR that Roland had procured just for this special occasion, then joins him on the couch. Roland presses the remote-control button, and the twenty-year-old surveillance tape of the elevator in the FXN building begins to play, without sound.

From a perspective directly behind and above, a stylishly dressed woman with a briefcase has positioned herself in the elevator. The woman presses the button for the thirty-ninth floor.

Before the doors close, a young man with a very large nose steps inside, smiles, and nods.

The doors close, and the elevator advances upward. As the button lights indicate the sixth, seventh, and eighth floors, the man appears to focus on the woman's breasts.

She turns slightly to address him.

The man seems genuinely upset about something, and in a shy way, indicates to the front of the woman's blouse.

The woman's face expresses her annoyance.

Again, the man indicates to her blouse.

The woman's annoyance turns to concern, and she questions the man.

The man points down the inside of his own shirt.

The woman's concern heightens, and her excited body language appears to ask a question.

He appears to answer.

She screams mutely for clarification.

The man nods.

The woman drops her briefcase and slaps at her blouse, mutely yelling for help.

The man steps forward and reaches down her blouse.

The fourteenth and fifteenth-floor buttons light up.

The woman holds her arms back to avoid impeding Robert Longpooper's efforts. Her movements suggest a growing hysteria.

He unbuttons her blouse, spreads it apart, and looks inside.

The woman mutely, but frantically, begs for his help.

He appears to suggest that some horrible creature may have crawled into her bra.

Button lights travel through the twentieth, twenty-first, and twenty-second floor as the woman's paranoia intensifies.

The man reaches into one side of her bra and withdraws a breast, which he quickly examines by holding it upwards by its nipple.

The woman pleads and implores with frenzied gestures.

The man immediately reaches back into her bra and withdraws her other breast and, also by holding it upwards by its nipple, is able to give it a thorough "once over" before indicating that the creature may have crawled down into her pants.

She silently screams for him to get it before it bites her private areas.

He unzips her pants, drops onto his knees in front of her, pulls her pants down, and with an urgent–yet thorough effort–brushes off all areas of skin between her breasts and her knees.

The thirty-ninth-floor button lights up and, as the woman is spasmodically shaking and jittering every part of her body while screaming mutely at the man who is on his knees with his arms stretched around her mid-section, slapping wildly at her buttocks . . . the elevator doors slide open.

And there, standing two-deep in front of the elevator, are the FXN CEO and its Board of Directors . . . with their mouths frozen open.

And then the elevator doors slide shut.

On the couch, Margaret stops the video and turns to Roland. "Well, that's him, Robert Gerald Longpooper. What do you think?"

Roland has begun to sweat–profusely. "Are you sure that's him?"

"I would recognize that nose anywhere."

There is an extended pause before Roland suddenly grabs his chest and keels over.

Panic-stricken, Margaret screams, drops to her knees and

cradles his pale face in her hands. "Darling! My darling! Please don't die!"

Weakly, Roland looks up into her eyes to say goodbye. But the strain is too great, and he can barely manage a few final words. "I am sorry, my precious one, but zee shock of realizing zat I muss keel a fellow human being–"

"No, my darling! You don't have to kill him. It no longer matters to me."

"But, I muss avenge zee brutalization of your innocence–"

"No, my darling. The Lord works in strange ways. If it had not been for Robert Longpooper, I would never have met you. Don't you see? Mr. Longpooper was simply–a messenger of the Lord."

Roland couldn't have said it better. "Yes, yes, now eet all makes sense. And I suddenly feel much better. I am going to lif!" He sits up. "Come to me, my leetle plum cake! Come to me now, my wife-to-be, and we shall lif and luf, and haff children, and leaf zis crazy movie business, and moof into zee peaceful solitude of zee desert, and lif under zee moon and zee stars! Oui?"

Margaret rests her hands on his chest. "Let us not be too hasty, my darling chef of sweet puddings. I am actually growing rather fond of this neighborhood."

CHAPTER TWENTY-FOUR

Eventually, Roland Valtrain and Margaret Bennington move out to a little farm in the desert, adopt a bunch of kids, and have a few chickens clucking around. They also have a very nice swimming pool surrounded by lovely gardens with babbling brooks running throughout.

At this point, it should be noted that as a result of the tenderness and joy that Margaret brought into Roland's life, he was finally able to understand the depth and harm of his peculiar need to fondle breasts at every possible opportunity.

And he vowed to repent for his history of inexcusably abhorrent behavior by committing the bulk of his vast fortune to eliminating the sexual abuse of women and children throughout the world.

And to begin with, Roland gave five hundred million dollars

to the"*ME TOO*" organization for the expressed purpose of building 'safe houses' in every state across the country.

He then gave the same amount to an international group of genetic-scientists, with instructions for them to find a way to eliminate the specific gene from the human DNA which enables the human species to engage in even the slightest sort of violent tendency.

Then, he and Margaret, working together, built a cozy little cottage on their property for Edward to live in while undergoing a very lengthy therapy designed to convince him that he is actually not an ostrich.

(Although many passersby still pull their cars off to the side of the road, next to the beautifully landscaped pastures, just to enjoy the sight of Edward strutting about.)

UPCOMING BOOKS FROM THE *"12 STORIES FROM THE CAMPFIRES OF MY MIND"* SERIES BY DAVID CREPS

1
KING BOSS

Even if you are naturally inclined to shrug off life's constant parade of disappointments by simply denying their ultimate relevance, what's your method for disregarding a doctor's assurance that you will be dead within a month? For Johnny James, the *King Boss*, it meant he had one last chance to live. Finally.

2
SWANKY SHAMPANE

This comedy set in Reno, Beverly Hills, and Malibu is the story of Best Actress nominee, Swanky Shampane, a two-timing, double-dealing, poetically-profane, ridiculously-neurotic, but fabulously charming, former cat house prostitute, obsessed with changing her public image prior to the night of the Academy Awards when she will be taking the front-row-center-seat next to her bitterest rival, "that filthy bitch" . . . Myrtle Street.

3
THE NEW YEARS RESOLUTION

A romantic comedy concerning the last two people a merciful God would ever put together under one roof, especially during the week that one of them is giving up cigarettes.

It's what happens when ridiculously neurotic egos do battle while under the pressures of a calm biological attraction.

4
THE OTHER BROTHERS

A Disney-style comedy about two twelve-year-old boys. One black. One white. One from the mean streets of Harlem, one from an isolated chicken farm in Nevada.

Both too young to be full-fledged con artists, but both already in abundant possession of the devilish charm and swagger necessary for the calling should their lives continue along their current paths.

And were it not for their love of basketball and their mutual respect for the way each other plays the game, these two big-talkers might never have made it to the brotherhood that bonds them into a lifetime of friendship.

5
MARGARITAVILLE

Is the story of two bungling con artists living on a pathetic excuse for a sailboat, in a trailer park, while looking for that one big score that will get them to the warm, turquoise waters and sandy, white beaches of the Caribbean, where they can live "just like Jimmy Buffet."

6
THE ROAD TO JACK'S HOUSE

The story of a thirty-six-year-old virgin who has a very assertive opinion on every matter under the sun. And the guy who, at the time of meeting this woman, is engaged in a search for the answer to the question, "What is the best way for me to live the rest of my life?"

They are both a little pissy, both a little self-righteous, and they each have their own personal agendas when they head down Highway 395 to take her screenplay to Hollywood, where she has good reason to believe that it will be read by Jack Nicholson. At his house. On a Saturday afternoon–while she is swimming in his pool, during a star-studded, rollicking-romp of a barbeque.

7
LAST CHANCE

A chilling comedy about the possibilities of "what if?"

What if the focus of present-day science were trained on finding a way to eliminate all violent tendencies from human behavior?

And what if a relatively small group of well-funded scientists undertook this problem, in secret, and through genetic engineering were successful in solving it?

And what if they not only discovered the formula for making the human a passive species, but at the same time realized a way to dispense this formula throughout the world–without notice and without permission? Should they?

8
THE GREATEST MOVIE EVER WRITTEN

The attempt by an artist of questionable sanity to write and direct a movie that will literally "save the world." The pressure is great. The time is short. And by every initial indication, his thinking is way too far "outside the box."

Yet he perseveres, fueled by a single belief: "You can't prevent the human race from destroying itself with a bigger, better weapon. But if your thoughts are crazy enough . . . you might be able to do it with an idea."

9
THE REUNION

The story of what happens when a thirty-year class reunion brings together five old high school friends who have been suffering from the same secret guilt from so many years ago.

It is also the story of what happens when Elizabeth Maryann Walker spends her weekend with these same five guys, up in the mountains, camping at Bennies Creek, falling in love for the second time in her life–with the same man.

10
THE IRONY OF IT ALL

A story of what might have happened during the last few weeks of the 2000 Presidential Election if the writer, Chesterfield Johnson, a man of unusual perceptions and bizarre solutions, had convinced candidate Al Gore to act in accordance with Chesterfield's unsolicited advice.

Besides his strategy to win Mr. Gore the election, Chesterfield has also devised a strategy to get his latest screenplay into the hands of an aging actress desperate to find a script worthy of her talent.

And within these dual tracks of Chesterfield's efforts, live an assortment of schemers and manipulators operating in the guise of Hollywood agents, political insiders, tabloid celebrities, and talk show hosts.

11
ON THE WALL IN THE CAVE

This comedy explores the absurdities of what can happen when a seemingly normal American man goes into a cave in the mountains to meditate on the problems of the world with the intention of figuring out the solution to the whole mess.

Current news headlines from any part of the world make this character's mindset very easy to understand.

12
THE SWEET REDEMPTION OF REPREHENSIBLE BOB

This is the story of a reprehensible human being with an insatiable need to fondle breasts at every possibility. With or without permission.

And the lovely woman who had suffered enormously for twenty years, before deciding to track him down and "shoot him through the eyeballs."

(Now available on *Amazon*)

ABOUT DAVID CREPS

David has worked as a ditch-digger, truck driver, dice-dealer, carpenter, screenwriter, playwright, and novelist.

The first highlight of his writing career happened when he was twenty-two years old, and Shecky Greene read a couple pages of his stuff, and said, "I've read worse."

And, in analyzing the unspoken words within Shecky's comment, David understood Shecky to mean, "Holy crap! I am the greatest writer Shecky has ever allowed to work for him for free!"

This was enough to inspire him through decades of laborious scribbling and ultimately provide him with enough cash to get a small mortgage on a cabin 8,000 feet up in the mountains, and to purchase a genuine 1966 greenish-gray (a color occasionally referred to, behind his back, as puke-green) U.S. Postal Service mail truck lined with wall-to-wall-to-ceiling-to-floor green shag carpet, which could transport more previously-used-assorted lengths of lumber in one haul than any vehicle in this entire country.

(David is also a husband, a father, a brother, a grandfather, a good-natured, and occasionally, totally innocent, rascal.)

www.ingramcontent.com/pod-product-compliance
Lightning Source LLC
Chambersburg PA
CBHW071313130626
46556CB00004B/1592